A THOUSAND SOULS

LEE NELSON

COUNCIL·PRESS™

Springville, Utah

ISBN: 1-55517-653-4
v.1

Published by Council Press
Imprint of Cedar Fort Inc.
www.cedarfort.com

Distributed by:

Typeset by Kristin Nelson
Cover design by Adam Ford
Cover design © 2002 by Lyle Mortimer
Printed in the United States of America
10 9 8 7 6 5 4 3 2 1

Printed on acid-free paper

Library of Congress Cataloging-in-Publication Data

Nelson, Lee.
  A thousand souls / by Lee Nelson.
    p. cm.
  ISBN 1-55517-653-4 (alk. paper)
  1. Mormon missionaries--Fiction. 2. Americans--Germany--Fiction. 3.
Young men--Fiction. 4. Germany--Fiction. I. Title.
  PS3564.E4675 T47 2002
  813'.54--dc21
                        2002007009

To my mother,

who never tires of my stories.

PROLOGUE

Mr. Crandall wasn't surprised when I showed up at his bank just before noon on a sunny Tuesday in March, 1965. I had been home from Germany only a few weeks, and like most returned missionaries, I was broke. I told him I needed three thousand dollars.

"Going to buy a car?" he asked.

"No sir."

"Student loans through the university have better interest rates if you need money for school," he said.

"I know, but it's not for school."

"An engagement ring?"

"Not that, either."

I told him I wanted to fly back to Germany to be the best man at a wedding, bless a baby and baptize a nun.

"An unusual request," he said, rubbing his chin, looking thoughtfully in my direction. "Twice, I sent money while you were in Germany. Those checks were donations for the work. But this is different. If I decide to give it to you, you will have to sign a note, and pay it back, with interest."

"I understand, sir."

"Do you have a job, or some other means to pay off the loan?"

"Not now, but I will when I return."

"Do you have any collateral?"

"Only a story."

"I don't suppose this would be the first time a banker

loaned money on a story," he smiled, wryly.

"It's a good one."

"They all are, when the object is to get money," he said. "Does it have anything to do with my donations to rent halls and buy newspaper advertising?"

"Sure does."

"I can hardly wait to hear it." He looked at his watch. "It's almost lunch time. I'll buy the food, and you tell the story."

"It's a deal," I said.

We walked down the street to a Chinese restaurant, found a table in the corner, and began a two-hour lunch where I gave him the condensed version of the events about to unfold.

ONE

Every Monday night my roommates and I cooked tacos, Tuesday spaghetti, Wednesday chicken, and on Thursday a huge pot of beef or mutton stew which was supposed to get us through the weekend. For breakfast each morning we had orange juice, cream of wheat and poached eggs on toast, exactly the same every morning. We were on our own for lunch. We paid six dollars each week into the grocery budget. There were four of us in the second-story apartment on Ashby Avenue in Berkeley, California. It was the spring of 1962, and we were freshmen at the University of California. The one who cooked the meals each day also washed the dishes the same night.

One Tuesday night when it was my turn to cook the spaghetti, I glanced at my watch as I sprinkled the last of the cayenne pepper into the bubbling pot of sauce. It was already seven and I had an appointment at eight with Bishop Kenner of the local student ward for Mormons.

My roommates—Steve, Dave and Syd—were already at the table, waiting for me to serve up supper. And since the designated cook for the night was also supposed to set the table, they were waiting for me to do that too. To pass the time they were having fast draw contests to see who was fastest at drawing a wooden match from his pocket and striking it on the zipper of his jeans. There was no benefit to

1

an of competition. I was the only Mormon
d the only one who didn't smoke.

ring everyone a glass of milk, I threw a handful
the table. As I drained the water off the noodles,
I   nced we were going to try something new. Since I
had an appointment and wouldn't have time to do the dishes,
I told them we were going to eat our spaghetti the way the
communists did.

Communism was popular in Berkeley at the time, especially on campus, and my comment immediately caught the
attention of my roommates who wanted to know how
communists ate spaghetti. They put their matches away.

With nothing but glasses of milk and forks on the vinyl
table, I proceeded to dump the noodles in a pile in the center.

"Why do the communists eat spaghetti this way?" Steve
asked.

"You've heard the slogans," I explained. "Everything in
common, no private ownership, everybody sharing. Eating
on separate plates is a selfish, capitalist idea."

"No kidding," Dave said.

Using a towel to protect my hands, I removed the boiling
pot of sauce from the stove and brought it to the table.

"Tonight we truly eat together," I said, pouring the entire
pot of steaming sauce over the pile of noodles. Quickly, I
handed everyone pieces of sliced white bread so they could
prevent tiny rivulets of red from running over the edge of the
table. Once the sauce was safely contained, we picked up
our forks—and after addressing each other as Comrade Syd,
Comrade Dave, Comrade Steve and Comrade Lee—we began
to eat. The only problem was the seam across the middle of

the table, some of the sauce seeped through to drip on the floor.

"What does the bishop want?" Syd asked when we were nearly finished.

"I think he wants to talk about me going on a mission," I said.

"Do you want to go?" Steve asked.

"I'm thinking about it," I said.

"It would kill me to go two years without a date," Dave added, offering me a cigarette. He did that frequently, though I always refused.

Syd started to say something, but Dave interrupted, "I know how you can get the bishop to leave you alone."

"How?"

"When you're sitting in his office tonight, just light up a cigarette and blow smoke in his face."

I got up from the table to begin cleaning things up so I could be off to my appointment. I was aware that my roommates were whispering behind my back but didn't pay any attention.

Suddenly I felt myself being tackled from behind. It was Dave, saying something about my being too religious. He was the biggest and strongest, had been a linebacker in high school. We tumbled out of the kitchen onto the living room carpet. Syd and Steve joined the attack. I had been through basic training in the Marine Corps reserve, and was taking a boxing class, but I was not a match for all three of them. Soon I was stretched out on my back, Steve and Syd holding my arms and legs, Dave sitting on top, announcing that a good Mormon boy was about to learn how to smoke.

He lit up a cigarette and shoved it between my lips. I spat it out, struggling unsuccessfully to get free. Dave persisted in pushing the cigarette in my mouth and I persisted in spitting it out. Though I was unable to squirm free, they were unable to make me smoke. I didn't like what was happening, and the temptation was to get angry, but these were my friends, my roommates, and they were just playing. I fought the urge to get mad. Then, almost before I knew what was happening, they let go of me and everyone got up. The fun was over. There were things to do. None of them seemed bothered that they had failed in their playful effort to make me smoke.

As we were laughing, catching our breath, tucking in our shirts—there was a loud thumping on the floor. Apparently our wrestling had been too noisy for the four junior and senior coeds who lived directly underneath us, and they were registering the usual complaint, tapping on their ceiling with broom handles.

"Maybe they wouldn't complain so much if they experienced some real noise," Steve whispered.

All four of us tiptoed into the bedroom Syd and I shared, to the closet where we stored the bars and free weights we used to build muscles. As quietly as possible, each of us picked up one of the 25-pound weights—inch-thick discs of solid iron about the size of large dinner plates—then tiptoed back to the living room.

With each of us holding a weight high above the head, Syd counted, "One, two, three." That's when we slammed the weights down on the floor, hoping to convince the coeds that the entire building was coming down on them. Then we scurried about to hide the weights and straighten up, knowing the apartment manager would soon be paying a visit.

"Don't forget to hang the rug on the door," Steve cautioned, not wanting the manager to see the result of one of our favorite study-avoidance past times—throwing butcher knives at the back side of the closed front door, often speculating what would happen if someone suddenly rushed in without knocking. We had more than enough money in our security deposit to buy a new front door, but didn't see any sense in hurrying up the day of reckoning.

When the apartment manager arrived, I was already down the stairs, headed for the street and my appointment with the bishop.

TWO

As I walked to class the next morning, I was thinking about my visit with the bishop. My hunch had been right. He asked me how I felt about going on a mission. I had turned nineteen in October. I said I didn't know if the church was true. I emphasized the word *know*. He encouraged me to pray about it. I promised him I would.

I was from the Walnut Creek area about twenty miles east of Berkeley. My family was active in the local ward. My father had served a mission in Denmark. While the subject of my going on a mission was sometimes talked about, my parents always said I didn't have to go if I didn't want to, but if I decided to go, they would be very happy to support me financially. I appreciated the fact that they didn't push, leaving the decision up to me.

I was on my way to Philosophy 101 that morning. As I entered campus from Telegraph Avenue, there was a bearded fellow standing by a tripod ringing a bell. His hair was long, and he wore leather sandals—an ordinary appearance at Berkeley in the early sixties. My parents would have called him a beatnik. On his tripod there was a map of the South Pacific, with an orange circle around the Christmas Islands where the U.S. government was testing nuclear bombs.

Being a few minutes early, I stopped to see what he

wanted. He said the nukes were destroying whales and porpoises, and poisoning the air and water with radioactive fallout. My first thought was to wonder how we were supposed to keep our defenses up against the Russians if we didn't test a bomb once in a while, but I didn't say anything.

He wanted me to give him money so a group of students could sail to the Christmas Islands, and in his words, "screw up" the government's program by planting themselves right smack in the middle of the testing area. They assumed the government would not blow up a bunch of college students. What caught my imagination was not the rightness or wrongness of the protest, but the sheer adventure of sailing off into the South Pacific with fellow students to stop the most powerful military on the face of the earth from exploding bombs on a remote uninhabited desert island. I donated a dollar to the cause before hurrying off to class.

Philosophy 101 was my favorite class that semester. We were reading works by Descartes, Hulme, Kant, even Darwin. A lot of students avoided philosophy because it was supposed to be hard, and I suppose it was. I didn't do very well on some of the tests, but I loved the reading assignments. Books were my best friends.

I remember flunking two classes in the eighth grade. The history teacher, a former Catholic priest named Marion St. John, took me aside one afternoon, saying he noticed that I was reading a lot of books that didn't have anything to do with school. He cautioned me not to let the pressure from the other teachers break my reading habit. He said if I continued to read so many books, I would become more educated than my classmates and teachers, even if I flunked the eighth grade. I remember promising him I would try harder in school.

In addition to fiction works, I had discovered the fascinating world of nonfiction too, like the time my friend Syd and I learned how to play poker. First, we used matches for money, then graduated to pennies.

One Saturday afternoon, his father noticed we were playing for money and decided to teach us a lesson about gambling. He asked if he could join us. We said he could on the condition he brought his own pennies. He was a smart man, an engineer, and soon won all our money. He seemed very pleased that he had taught two boys a lesson on the dangers of gambling.

A few days later, I was rambling through the stacks at the local library when I discovered a book about poker, written by a man named Hoyle. I checked it out, read it twice and made a pile of notes. Needless to say, I didn't do very well in school that week. I was learning probability theory, the odds of drawing any card or combinations of cards while playing poker, and utilizing those odds as part of playing strategies. I learned how to pull off a successful bluff, too.

After discussing the Hoyle book with Syd, we approached his father, saying we hadn't learned our lesson on the dangers of gambling well enough, inviting him to play with us again. This time the outcome was different. After losing three or four dollars, the father kindly excused himself. Yes, books were my friends.

In addition to the reading assignments in the philosophy class, I also loved the classroom discussions. The teacher, Professor Anderson, was young with sandy hair, freckles, and a harelip. His b's sounded like m's. I wondered too if he might be colorblind. Sometimes he would wear a pink shirt and brown tie with a green sport coat. But his handicaps didn't go beyond pronunciation and color selection. In our numerous class debates, Mr. Anderson was always the winner.

And I figured it would be class as usual this particular winter day, but I was wrong. He began class, asking if anyone *knew* there was a God. He asked for a show of hands.

I didn't raise mine. I wasn't being cowardly, either. I'd told Bishop Kenner the night before, I didn't *know* if there was a God, or if the Church was true, though I believed these things to be true. After reading Descartes and Hulme, about all I knew for sure was how to play poker.

There were about two hundred students in the class with seven or eight raising their hands in response to his question. He called on a pretty blond girl near the front to explain herself. When she had difficulty, he started asking her questions. Had she seen God? No. Had she heard his voice? No. Had she touched him? No. Had she smelled him? No. Then how could she know? He only laughed when she said her parents and grandparents had taught her about God.

"I suppose if they told you the world was flat, you would *know* that too," he chided. He called on several more students who couldn't explain their beliefs any better than the first girl.

Professor Anderson then told about a student, one time, who claimed to have heard the voice of God. Anderson had asked the student how he knew he wasn't dreaming, hallucinating, or just imagining the voice? He ended the story by telling us, "Even if you saw God, you don't know for sure. No one knows there's a God."

Professor Anderson talked a lot about God that semester. I don't think his goal was to destroy faith, as much as it was to get students to think for themselves and not just accept what they had been told. Professor Anderson didn't know if there was a God, and was convinced no one else knew either. None of the students could successfully stand up to him to defend their positions, though some tried.

How could I go on a mission if I didn't *know* if their was a God? That would make me a hypocrite. How could I devote two years of my life teaching a doctrine I didn't know for sure to be true? I thought a lot about these questions that winter.

I attended institute and church meetings at the local ward house. The bishop and others taught interesting classes in Mormon history and doctrine, though I was never fully satisfied with their handling of philosophical questions, like how you can really *know* if there's a God.

I remember a young woman who attended the Institute classes. Her name was Nancy. I don't ever remember being introduced to her, and I don't think we ever had a one-on-one conversation that lasted more than a few sentences, though I remember several group conversations. I would sit two or three rows behind her, trying not to look at her too much. I suppose there were other girls more beautiful, even more shapely, but there was something about this Mormon girl that put her five levels above the coeds my roommates dated, the ones who smoked and used four-letter words and who were willing to conclude a good date in the bedroom.

Even from three rows behind, I thought I could sense her innocence, her unblemished beauty, the purity of heart that made her irresistible. Though I never asked her for a date, I knew I would have gladly given my life in her defense, and sometimes fantasized doing just that. I had met other girls in my home town that stimulated similar feelings. These were the kind of people I wanted to be around, much more so than the Professor Andersons who debated philosophy, and the long-haired beatnik headed for the Christmas Islands.

As I considered going on a mission, I thought about the time I attended the dedication of the Tri-Stake Center in Oakland. I was in the back row of the huge auditorium when the aging prophet, David O. McKay, then in his nineties, hobbled across the stage to speak. Another man was holding his arm as he took six-inch steps. He was so old and frail, I didn't know if he would be able to say anything.

As President McKay shuffled across the stage to the podium, the congregation began singing, *We Thank Thee O God, For A Prophet*. I remember the strong, burning feeling in my chest, the choking in my throat, the tears streaming down my cheeks. By Professor Anderson's definition, I couldn't know on an intellectual level that this old man was a prophet of God, but I could sure feel it, in a very powerful way.

I had that same feeling sometimes when reading the *Book of Mormon*. I had read the book twice, before my nineteenth birthday. In addition to being a fascinating history of the early inhabitants on the American continent, including stories of their wars and conflicts, there were also accounts of spiritual strivings and manifestations that caused that same warm, choked-up feeling deep inside me.

I suppose the decision to go on a mission boiled down to a struggle between my intellect—with plenty of classroom coaching from Professor Anderson—and my warm feelings toward an aging prophet, a beautiful young woman and a strange, but fascinating book. In the end, it was my heart that won the battle. That spring I told the bishop that, though I still didn't know if the Church was true, I believed it was, and would go on a mission if the Church would have me.

THREE

Following the next stake conference, I had an interview with the visiting general authority, Elder McConkie from Salt Lake City. When he asked if I had a preference on where I would like to serve, I told him I would like to go to the southwest Indians in Arizona or New Mexico. I had read a number of books about Apaches and Navajos, and thought I would like to work among these people. I could see myself galloping from village to village on a black stallion, blessing their sick and teaching in their native tongue. I explained some of this to the general authority. He listened quietly, then underlined the part on the application that said I had three years of Spanish in high school.

Several weeks later I received a letter, signed by President David O. McKay, calling me to serve in the South German Mission for two-and-a-half years. So much for visiting hogans on horseback.

The next few weeks my mother spent her time doing what all missionary mothers seem to like to do, getting her son outfitted to go—buying suits, shirts, ties, luggage, underwear, handkerchiefs, socks, overcoats, hats, and dozens of other items—the general assumption being that I would not visit a store in two-and-a-half years. At the farewell meeting at church, I felt awkward—struggling to verbalize the transition from son and student to minister of the gospel.

After a tearful departure, I found myself at the mission home in Salt Lake City, where all new missionaries at that time spent a week before leaving to their fields of labor. At that time the church did not conduct language training classes for missionaries. Nobody called me Lee anymore, just Elder Nelson, or Elder.

The mission home in those days was an old stucco building several blocks north of the Salt Lake Temple. There were about 200 in our group, including sister missionaries and older couples. We lived in a dormitory arrangement. I shared a room with five elders also bound for South Germany.

We received our meals at the Hotel Utah several blocks away. I don't think the cook was a student of modern scripture, at least not the 89th Section of the *Doctrine & Covenants* which prescribes the Mormon health code and its caution against heavy meat consumption, especially in hot weather. It was August, with the thermometer soaring into the high nineties and low hundreds every afternoon. For breakfast we received generous servings of bacon and sausage, and at other meals, huge piles of fried chicken, roast beef, chicken fried steak and stuffed pork chops. I suppose they were trying to fatten us up before sending us out into the cruel world, but in the extreme heat, without exercise, dressed in three-piece suits, sitting in classrooms most of the day, I felt like a stuffed turkey most of the time.

It occurred to me that I might push the meat away and eat like the *Word of Wisdom* prescribed, but having the appetite of a healthy nineteen-year-old, I decided living the letter of the health law could wait until I arrived in Germany.

I remember one evening wondering if this neglect toward the *Word of Wisdom* might be a sin. But when they brought in the stuffed pork chops, I decided to resolve the question later.

The mission home was managed by an older couple, Brother and Sister Richards. I remember Sister Richards as a huge grandmother bear of a woman whose only mission in life, it seemed, was to make new missionaries feel welcome and loved. She did it by ambushing us at the front door, throwing her huge arms around any one of us, and squeezing with all her might. She reminded me of a little girl hugging kittens and puppies. She tried to hug each missionary every day, physically squeezing the loneliness and homesickness away. She succeeded, at least with me.

We spent much of the week in classrooms, receiving instruction. There were talks by recently returned missionaries, young men just two years older than I was. I marveled, not so much about what they said, as their ability to get up in front of a group without the benefit of notes, and speak with eloquence and conviction. I had given lots of talks in church, and even taken a public speaking class in college, but I could not speak without notes, finding it almost impossible to think on my feet—for me, every word had to be thought out in advance. But it wasn't that way with these returned missionaries. Abundant beautiful words flowed effortlessly out of their mouths in an endless stream of wisdom and knowledge. I wondered if that gift of speech would be given to me, the young man who was too shy most of the time to ask a girl for a date. Such a gift alone would make the mission worthwhile.

During the week, we were ushered in groups over to the church office building to be set apart by general authorities. I was assigned to Spencer W. Kimball, then a member of the quorum of twelve apostles.

Elder Kimball was from Arizona and had a keen interest in the various southwest Indian tribes. His office was full of pottery, blankets, primitive bows and arrows, and Indian art. As I waited to be set apart, I couldn't help but think back on my request to go to the Indians. Still, I couldn't deny a growing excitement about going to Germany.

Elder Kimball invited me to sit in a cushioned straight-backed chair in the center of an open area. He and I were the only ones in his office. Stepping behind me, he laid his warm, strong hands on my head and in a raspy voice, proceeded to set me apart as a missionary. He blessed me that I would be protected from harm, that I would enjoy good health, and that if I kept the commandments and remained faithful I would be instrumental in bringing *a thousand souls* to the truth.

I didn't hear anything else. I had talked to missionaries who had gone to Germany. None had baptized more than a handful of people. Some hadn't baptized any. The German missions were among the toughest in the Church. Didn't Elder Kimball know that? Of course he did. Why then did he say I would help a thousand souls come to the truth? Things like that didn't happen in the twentieth century. I was not Wilford Woodruff, who had baptized entire congregations while on a mission to England.

I felt a surge of emotion in my chest. When he finished the blessing I wanted to ask him about the promise, but other missionaries were waiting to be blessed too. As I shook Elder Kimball's firm hand, I could feel his goodness and warmth. I hoped with all my heart he was inspired, but as I left his office that day I felt a new burden resting on my shoulders. If I didn't keep the commandments and have enough faith, perhaps *a thousand souls* would be denied the gospel. What a terrible burden to place on the shoulders of a young man who was slow of speech, and didn't even *know* the church was true. I decided I would have to live on faith— just do what was right and maybe, just maybe, the Lord would guide me in the paths I should follow.

I learned the next morning that life was not that simple. Another elder and I were walking along the sidewalk on the east side of Temple Square on our way to breakfast at Hotel Utah, when a stranger in shabby clothes asked if he could speak to me. I stopped.

The man said he lacked two dollars in being able to buy a bus ticket to return to his family in North Dakota. He asked if I could spare that much. I gave him the money, and quickly received a scolding from my companion, who said the man had suckered me into giving him money for liquor, that the story about needing the bus ticket was a sham to part me from my money. My companion insisted I had done the wrong thing, that I indulged the man's alcohol habit. I disagreed.

As we stopped at the red light, waiting to cross over to the hotel, we were approached by another man asking for money. I think he saw me give the two dollars to the first man. The second man wanted a dollar to buy some breakfast. Before I could reach into my pocket to get the money, my companion entered the conversation, telling the man we would not give him any money, but if he wished to join us for breakfast, we would be glad to share our food with him. To my surprise, the man declined the invitation. We crossed the street without him, my companion proud at having taught me a lesson.

In my remaining days at the mission home, I was approached by more people asking for money. On the one hand, I didn't want to pay for booze or encourage shoddy behavior. But on the other hand I didn't want to become insensitive to the needs of the poor and needy, and these people were certainly poor and in need of something. I continued to give some of them money, against the protests of the elder who had tried to teach me a lesson, but I was no longer certain I was doing right. The only thing I had learned for sure was that being righteous is not as simple as it seems.

I concluded life was like the *Word of Wisdom*. While some things were black and white, like abstaining from using alcohol and tobacco, other things were gray, like deciding whether or not to eat stuffed pork chops on a hot summer afternoon. I hoped I would gain the wisdom to be able to handle the gray areas.

My stay at the mission home ended two days before my scheduled departure for Germany. Knowing I would be in the company of companions continually for the next two and a half years I decided to spend part of the last day by myself.

The next afternoon, at my grandfather's farm in West Bountiful, I saddled a tall bay gelding, a horse that was almost impossible to mount unless someone else was holding the bridle. My grandfather had purchased it from a schoolteacher who couldn't handle it. It needed calming; the kind that can only come through wet saddle blankets and long rides.

I headed out onto the Farmington Bay bird refuge, galloping along the endless miles of dirt roads that criss-crossed the vast marshlands where flocks of yellow-winged blackbirds, sea gulls, and coots squawked and fluttered as I galloped past. The hot, dry wind blowing in off the salt flats felt good against my face and arms. The horse was eager to cover the miles, his coat glistening with sweat. It was hard to believe that in three days I would be walking along the cobbled lanes of southern Germany seeking *a thousand souls* to join what I believed to be the only true church on the face of the earth.

FOUR

The South German Mission home in the 1960s was not the typical mission home. It was a mansion; a small castle, located on a hill in Feurbach, a suburb of Stuttgart. The estate comprised several acres surrounded by tall stone fences. The cobblestone driveway led to a heavy steel and wood front gate that looked like it might stop a tank. The multi-car garage was separate from the main house and included servants' quarters where some of the mission staff lived. There were circular staircases, an indoor swimming pool converted to a mission office, walk-in refrigerator, and high ceilings with hand-carved crown moldings everywhere. It was the kind of place where the Rockefellers and Vanderbilts would feel at home.

The mission president was Blyth M. Gardner, a rancher and businessman from Richfield, Utah. He had the looks and bearing of an IBM senior vice president—perfect in appearance, articulate and intense. I was a little surprised that he drove a maroon Buick, shipped over from the United States, rather than a Mercedes Benz. The mission home was located only a few miles from the Mercedes Benz factory.

Each of the five new elders had a private interview with President Gardner before he decided where we would go, and more importantly, who our first companions would be.

I remember walking into his office, shaking hands and

sitting down. I had never been so intimidated in my life, and I don't know why, only that my hands were wet, and if I tried to answer any of his questions with more than a yes or no I seemed to stammer like a fool. I couldn't point my finger at any one thing that made me feel that way.

He said we couldn't go swimming, attend movies, or ever be alone except when taking a bath or going to the bathroom. If we went to the corner to mail a letter or pick up a liter of milk, we were to be together. Only handshakes were allowed with female members, no hugging or touching of any kind. No rides in privately-owned vehicles. We were to wear our suits, including coats, at all times, except for a three-hour period Friday morning—our diversion day. We weren't to sleep in past six in the morning, even on Sundays, and never stay up later than ten-thirty at night, when the Holy Ghost went to bed. We were not to leave our assigned areas without permission from the mission president. We were to write home once a week, no more, no less, and we weren't supposed to write to girlfriends more than once a month. We were not allowed to put pictures of girlfriends on the walls of our apartments, or by our beds. We weren't to call home more than once a year, but at $22 a minute that wasn't supposed to be a problem. We were expected to wear hats from November through March, no exceptions. We were not to eat with members more than once a week, and never stay longer than an hour. I suppose they needed all those rules to keep 200 nineteen-year-olds in line.

The more scary part of the interview was not the talk about things we couldn't do, but President Gardner's description of what we were expected to do. After arising at six we were to pray, shave and dress. We were to be seated at a table and begin studying by six thirty. For an hour, we studied alone, then for an hour, we studied with our companion, usually reading scriptures or reviewing discussions in German. After that, we ate breakfast and planned our day. At nine, we were to be out on the streets talking to people. He called this *proselyting*. We were *proselytors* who went from door to door, conducted street meetings and taught people in their homes. We had a half hour off for lunch, and one hour for dinner. We weren't supposed to return home until nine at night. This was our expected schedule Monday through Saturday, except for the three-hour diversion period from nine to twelve on Friday mornings when we were supposed to write home, do laundry, take our weekly bath, shop for groceries, work out or play basketball. If we had any time left, we could take pictures or go sightseeing. On Sundays, we were expected to proselyte when not in church. We were expected to tally sixty-five hours of proselyting time every week. We were to keep track of our time in fifteen-minute intervals on weekly reports which we sent to the mission office. He said he read every one of them.

We were expected to memorize, word-for-word, a two-minute door approach, a fifteen-minute screening discussion, and the standard six missionary lessons, each one averaging about an hour in length—in German, of course. If I remember correctly, the first lesson, alone, comprised over twenty single-spaced pages in the missionary manual.

I left his office wondering if I had made a mistake coming

on a mission. I didn't know if I could follow so many rules. Basic training in the Marine Corps looked easy next to this. I didn't know if I could get the spirit of the Lord to be with me if I was smothered under too many restrictions. But I guessed if others were doing all of that, maybe I could too. But maybe I couldn't, what then? I wondered if missionaries ever got ulcers, or suffered from nervous breakdowns. I learned later they did.

As we sat down to dinner that evening with President Gardner's family and staff, we were told there would be no English spoken at the table. Lively conversations were going on all around, but I couldn't understand anything that was being said. I had purchased a German-English dictionary earlier in the day and was told if I looked up every new word I heard I would soon be speaking German.

Pulling my dictionary from my pocket I gave it a try. Everyone was speaking so fast I couldn't catch one in a thousand words. When I finally did succeed in singling out a word, I couldn't find it in the dictionary.

I remember one native German sister who was working in the mission home. She was pretty—short brown hair, sparkling eyes, perfect complexion and figure. Her words just rolled effortlessly forth—soothing, guttural sounds like a babbling brook. I couldn't single out any specific words. They all just flowed together like music from her beautiful mouth. Others laughed at what she said, so I assumed they understood. Maybe I would too, some day. I was scared.

Early the next morning, they gave me a small binder called the *Black Book* which contained a door approach in the form of a three-question survey, and the fifteen-minute screening discussion. After a member of the mission staff sold me his bicycle, they herded me onto a train and shipped me off to Singen, a town of about thirty thousand people near Germany's southern border with Switzerland. The elders who put me on the train advised me to study the door approach in the front of the *Black Book* because I would be giving it before the day was through. My hands were shaking as I opened the binder to look at the pictures and study the survey questions.

The German countryside was beautiful, neat little farms among endless rolling hills and patches of green trees. It was August, and the farmers were putting up hay. There were no mowing and bailing machines like in Utah and California. Because Germany had lots of rain, the farmers couldn't leave their freshly-cut hay in rows on the ground like in America. They stacked it by hand on tripods made of wooden poles. Then when it was dry they carried it in wagons to their barns.

It was late afternoon when the train arrived at the Singen station. I was met by my new companion, Elder Zollinger from Logan, Utah. He was tall, thin, and soft-spoken. He balanced my suitcase on the handlebars of his bike and headed up the cobblestone street. I followed on my new bicycle. Our living quarters consisted of a single upstairs room. There was a toilet down the hall, no shower.

My desire to take a day, or two or three, to unpack my things was not to be. Before I could even get my suitcase open, Elder Zollinger announced that I could unpack later. It was still early in the day and we were going tracting. We rode to the outskirts of town where we parked our bikes under a tree.

Elder Zollinger pulled a small green notebook out of his pocket and wrote down the address of the first house. After returning the tracting book to the inside pocket of his suit coat, we walked up the steps to the first door.

I looked closely at my companion as he reached out to knock. There was no fear in his eyes, no trembling hand. His knuckles tapped on the door with firmness and confidence. I prayed no one was home. Elder Zollinger knocked again. I was ready to begin our retreat down the steps when the door finally swung open.

Standing before us was an older woman, maybe fifty with huge, broad shoulders, perhaps a professional wrestler in her younger years. She was frowning. I looked at her hands to make sure she was not holding a weapon. My companion said something in German. She responded. I couldn't catch any of the words. Before Elder Zollinger could open his *Black Book* to show her the pictures, she closed the door.

"See, that wasn't so bad," he said as we backed down the steps. I didn't respond.

At the next house, Zollinger knocked loudly, then turned to me. "Your turn," he said, handing me the *Black Book*.

"I don't speak German yet," I choked.

"No better place to learn." He knocked a second time. He was serious about me asking the survey questions. In vain I tried to remember the first question.

Suddenly the door swung wide. A middle-aged man was standing before us, partly bald with an extended paunch, wearing only a T-shirt and work pants, no shoes. Like the woman at the last house, he was not happy to see us. I thought if I said nothing, Elder Zollinger would have to initiate the conversation. I was wrong. The man looked at me, then at Elder Zollinger, then back at me. I smiled. The man did not smile back. The silence seemed eternal. My face felt red and I thought I could feel sweat dripping from the ends of my finger tips.

To my amazement, the survey questions were suddenly on the tip of my tongue. I opened the *Black Book*, showed the man the color photo of the Swiss temple, and asked, *"Ist dieser temple für sie ein Begriff?"* I did it without any help from my companion. I smiled at the man. Instead of answering my question about the temple, he turned to Elder Zollinger, said something in German, then closed the door.

"What did he say?" I asked. "Why didn't he answer my question?"

"He said he was very impressed with your presentation, but doesn't have time to talk right now." I sensed my companion was not telling the truth.

"Thanks for being nice, but tell me what he really said."

"He said he didn't understand English."

"But I was speaking German."

"He didn't know that. We need to work on your accent."

We visited about a dozen homes that first day. Because it was evening, most people were home. If they answered the first question about recognizing the Swiss temple, we explained that it was the Mormon temple in Switzerland. Then we asked the second question, wanting to know how much they knew about the Mormons. If they answered that, we asked if they would like to know more. After each response, we made a mark in the book, keeping track of our survey results. We continued taking turns, and some of the people seemed to understand what I was saying, but I couldn't be sure because I couldn't understand what they were saying back. None of the people invited us in, but one woman asked us to come back the next evening when her husband would be home.

"So this is tracting," I thought as we headed back to our bikes. "I can do this. Maybe missionary work won't be so hard after all."

That evening as I was unpacking my suitcase and arranging my things, I noticed that Elder Zollinger was cleaning up his *Black Book*, erasing the response marks we had made after asking the questions.

"You forgot to record the results before erasing them," I said, trying to be helpful.

"We don't keep track," he said. "It's not a real survey."

"We told the people we were conducting a survey."

"We are. We just don't keep track of the results."

"Why not?"

"We don't care about the results. We're just using the survey to get people to talk to us, to get our toe in the door."

"We deceived those people."

"No, we didn't. We asked questions and wrote down the answers. That's a survey. It's their problem if they think the results go into some giant computer so reporters from the New York Times can look at the results and write stories on how people in southern Germany feel about the Mormons."

I didn't say any more. What did I know? I had been in Germany only a few days.

I thought about Karl Maeser, who was probably the most famous German convert of all time. He helped found

Brigham Young University. He said that if someone put him behind prison walls, he would try to get out, and might succeed, but if someone drew a circle around him, on the ground, and got him to promise not to step outside the circle, he would die before crossing the line. I didn't think Maeser would conduct a phony survey.

When Zollinger's alarm clock sounded at six the next morning, we jumped out of bed, said our prayers, washed, shaved, dressed and did some pushups. At six thirty, we were seated at a table engaged in an hour of individual study. I was supposed to be memorizing the screening discussion and ten vocabulary words Elder Zollinger had written by hand on green index cards. At seven thirty, we began reading the *Book of Mormon* together, in German. He would read five verses, then it was my turn. He corrected my pronunciation and once in a while asked me to explain the meaning of certain words. If I couldn't do it, he wrote the words on the green cards.

At eight-thirty, we boiled up a pan of water on a hotplate, poured in some rolled wheat and a few handfuls of raisins, dried apples, and two raw eggs. A few minutes later we poured the steaming contents into two bowls, then poured yogurt and sugar over the top. Not bad. At nine, we were headed back to our tracting area.

Not as many people were home. We visited a lot of houses, making a few more appointments for screening discussions. One old woman even let us in. Elder Zollinger gave her the screening discussion on the spot. When he was finished, she said something about being Catholic, gave us each a piece of *Apfel Strüdle*, and sent us on our way.

Between houses, there was plenty of time to talk. Elder Zollinger told me about his mission and his home in Logan. I told him about college at Berkeley and basic training in the Marines. I felt lucky to have such a good companion. At noon, I was ready to stop. My feet hurt.

We rode our bikes to a little restaurant where we found seats on wooden benches at the end of a long table. Strewn along the top of the table were dozens of cardboard coasters with beer advertisements printed on them. I couldn't read the menu, and felt too tired to struggle with the dictionary, so when the waitress came to take our order, I asked Elder Zollinger to order for me. That was a mistake.

When my lunch arrived, I recognized the boiled potatoes, thinly sliced and covered with chopped onions and vinegar water, but I did not recognize the main dish, little pink slippery things swimming in a light brown gravy.

"What's this?" I asked.

"Bitte?"

It looked like it might be lobster or scallops, so I tried one. Definitely not fish. "I would like to know what I am eating?" I demanded.

"Bitte?"

"Why won't you tell me?"

"How bad do you want to learn the language?" he asked.

"About as bad as I want to wash this terrible taste out of my mouth," I said.

"Do you want me to help you?"

"Of course."

"Then from now on we speak German and only German. That's the single best thing I can do to help you learn the language."

"OK, but tell me what I'm eating."

"Bitte?"

Finally, I understood what he was doing. I thought a minute.

"Was ist das?" I said, pointing to my plate.

"Nieren."

I opened my dictionary and learned I was eating chopped kidney. While eating my potatoes, I opened the menu and looked up more words. I found brains and liver, also pork, beef, veal, venison and chicken.

After finishing his chunk of what appeared to be deep fried pork, Elder Zollinger felt sorry for me with only boiled potatoes, so he ordered two *Butter Pretzele.* I had had pretzels before, but never anything like these. They were huge, hard-crusted on the outside, but soft and chewy on the inside. The waitress sliced the pretzels in two, sideways, and smeared on about a quarter inch of white, low-salt butter across the entire surface area of the bottom half, then placed the other half on top of the butter. I could have eaten three or four. So good.

"If you know what to order, there are a lot of good things to eat here," he said.

"Bitte?" I responded.

FIVE

A few days later, all thirteen Singen missionaries fasted and prayed at the same time. The purpose was to enjoy more success in the area. Even with thirteen missionaries, there had not been a baptism in Singen in many months. At the end of the day, we rode our bikes to the chapel to end our fast with the other missionaries, ten elders and three sisters. The chapel was a gray two-story apartment-like building at the end of an alley, with two or three classrooms and a chapel large enough to hold thirty or forty people. The only one not present at the meeting was the district leader, Elder Horlacher.

I was pleasantly surprised when one of the sister missionaries said he was up on the Howentviel, a small mountain at the edge of town, with ancient rock remains of fortresses and crumbling battlements at the top of it. People hiked up there on weekends and holidays, but this was the middle of the week

I figured that, fasting like the rest of us, Elder Horlacher had gone to the top of the mountain to seek a special blessing from the Lord. In my mind's eye I could see him kneeling on the highest rock, pleading our needs and wants to the Lord of Israel. Our district leader was a spiritual giant. Because of him the Lord would bless us. Soon we would be baptizing. Wow, it was great to be a missionary.

I was surprised the other missionaries seemed so nonchalant over the spiritual endeavors of our leader. There was talk of transfers, news from home, and a lot of interest in an elder whose mother had sent him a jar of American peanut butter. I wished I were up on the Howentviel with Elder Horlacher.

After the prayer to end our fast, some of the missionaries began a heated discussion about the missionary-sponsored youth programs in England, where thousands of young people were apparently being baptized. The elders would play soccer or basketball with the children, then invite them over to the church for soda and cookies. The elders would tell the kids about their church which was like a *sports club* with an initiation requirement. Instead of eating a raw egg, or something like that, kids who wanted to join had to be dunked in the baptismal font. Thousands of children were joining the Church without the consent of their parents, and without going through the prescribed lesson material.

My first thought was that perhaps this was how I would see the fulfillment of Elder Kimball's blessing, that I would be instrumental in bringing thousands to the truth. I would do youth programs. Before I could get very excited about it, however, Elder Zollinger cautioned me by saying Church leaders frowned on people joining for any reasons other than legitimate religious conversion, and that parental consent for youth converts was mandatory. He didn't think the youth programs in England, or those beginning in Germany, would be around very long.

"Germany?" I asked.

"Sure," he said. "What do you think Elder Horlacher is

doing on the Howentviel?"

"I thought..."

He burst my bubble by explaining that our leader was experimenting with a youth program too, that instead of fasting and praying like the rest of us, he had taken his youth soccer group up on the mountain for a weenie roast.

While we were ending our fast with prayer, our leader was explaining the initiation requirement of baptism to a bunch of hungry ten-year-olds. I was so disappointed, so disillusioned. I felt foolish too, and was glad I hadn't expressed what I was thinking to the other missionaries.

The next morning as we were beginning to tract in a new area, we opened a front gate so we could approach a house which was fenced in by a stone wall. A huge black dog came bounding around the side of the house, headed straight for us, snarling and growling. We stepped back from the gate, too late to run, just as the dog lunged to clear the stone wall. That's when he hit the end of the chain we had not noticed earlier. The dog was jerked over backwards, but continued to bark and growl at us. We made no effort to enter the yard, but in the days to come, we went out of our way to go by that same house. There was a certain morbid fascination in watching that slobbering monster charge at us, fully intending to kill us, then at the last second get jerked back as he hit the end of the chain.

Then one day as the dog was flipped over backwards, the chain snapped. The dog was free to get us. The wall was only a meter high. We were dead meat. We were sorry we had taunted the dog, and were now going to pay dearly for our mistake. We braced ourselves for the attack we knew would come. We were too close to think we could outrun the huge dog.

But as the dog scrambled back on his feet, suddenly realizing he was no longer restrained by the chain, he didn't know what to do. Apparently he had never been beyond the area defined by the chain. Now that he was free to enter unknown territory, he was afraid to do it. Instead of attacking us, he retreated to his former hiding place around the side of the house. We were amazed and grateful, at the same time.

As we talked about it, we figured there had to be a lesson about human behavior here somewhere. We decided that people, like the mean dog, frequently set boundaries for themselves, beyond which they are unable to go.

I remembered when I was eleven years old. It seemed everyone I knew was playing a one-person board game called *IQ*. As I remember, the game board contained forty-eight holes, forming a cross, each arm containing three rows of holes. Little pegs, two blue and the rest red, were placed in the holes leaving one empty hole in the center. You jumped one peg over another so it could land in an empty hole, then you removed the peg that had been jumped over, like in *Checkers*. The object was to remove as many of the pegs as possible.

The instructions on the box said that if you could play until five or six pegs remained, you had a normal IQ. If only three or four remained, you had an above-average IQ. If one or two remained, your intelligence was near genius level. If you could play until only one blue peg remained in the center position, then Albert Einstein had better move over because he was no longer the smartest person in the world.

I had played the game off and on for about six months, and my best score was three remaining pegs. No matter how hard I played, I could never do any better. Then one day I was having lunch with my grandparents on a lazy summer afternoon when one of their friends stopped by to visit, a retired medical doctor, probably in his mid-seventies. He saw the IQ game on the table and asked if he could give it a try. I returned the pegs to the holes and pushed the board in front of him.

My guess was that he would end up with about four pegs—being a doctor and all. Casually I watched his hand as he jumped and removed pegs. There was nothing in his manner that caused me to think he might do better than I could do. Almost before I realized it, he was through, one red peg left in the center position. According to the instructions on the box, he was as smart as Albert Einstein.

"Impossible," I said. "Nobody is supposed to do that, except Albert Einstein."

"I did," he smiled.

"You must have cheated. Do it again."

"I didn't cheat. You know that, you were watching."

"Do it again."

"No. You do it."

"I have never done less than three pegs, usually four or five."

"Then learn to do it with one left in the middle."

"But it says on the box. . ."

"That was written by marketing guys who want to sell stuff."

"I have never seen anyone until now do less than three."

"I guess too many people believe the instructions on the box."

"You don't?"

"Of course not. It's a simple problem. You just try different strategies and systems until you find one that works. Not nearly as tough as some of the calculus problems you'll get in college. Just trial and error until you get it right. Get a system or strategy so that you can remember when you finally get one left in the middle, how you did it."

"Show me."

"No. You're a smart kid. Figure it out yourself." After saying that, he got up from the table and left.

My whole opinion of the game had changed. A simple math problem? We'll see. Within half an hour I figured out a system that enabled me to end up with a blue peg in the center hole every single time. I knew I was no Einstein. Later I realized I was just like that dog in Reutlingen who didn't know there was a world beyond the end of his chain. The marketing guys for the game had written a chain of words that held people in check just like the chain on the dog. The doctor showed me how to break the chain. My mind was churning, already planning how I would take that game to school in the fall and use it to improve my financial situation with lunchtime wagers.

Elder Zollinger and I wondered if our daily tracting routine might be like that chain too. Maybe there was a better way to find and teach people, but we just couldn't see it.

We talked about a lot of things as we tracted the streets

of Singen. Sometimes I asked for permission to speak in English until a certain subject matter was discussed to completion. We had a lot of time for such discussion because few of the South German Catholics wanted to talk to us.

One morning I asked Zollinger about the workings of German politics. He said the only thing most missionaries knew about government was that West Germany's chancellor, Conrad Adenauer, (Add-an-hour) had invented daylight savings.

The next week we had another district meeting at the church. President and Sister Gardner drove down from Stuttgart to be with us when we ended another day of fasting with a testimony meeting and prayer. After the president and his wife gave brief remarks, the meeting was opened up for the testimonies of the missionaries. Elder Horlacher went first, bearing a fervent and enthusiastic testimony. The rest of the elders and sisters followed, one at a time, giving thanks for the privilege to serve the Lord. There was no mention made of Elder Horlacher's youth program, but every elder and sister said they *knew* the Church was true, that Joseph Smith was a true prophet, and that Jesus was the Christ. I still couldn't say I *knew* those things, though I believed, so I decided not to say anything at all. I felt ashamed that I didn't *know* like the rest of them.

After all the other missionaries had given their testimonies, there was a long pause. Elder Horlacher glanced over his shoulder at me. So did some of the other missionaries. Everyone knew I was the only one who had not done it. But I had made up my mind. Until I could *know* like the rest of them, I wouldn't stand up and say something less worthy.

It seemed to me the silence of the meeting lasted at least an hour, though it was probably only a few minutes. Some of the elders and sisters stared at me like I was some kind of freak. The pressure was intense, but I had survived basic training in the Marine Corps, so I guessed I could also survive this.

I half expected President Gardner to order me to give my testimony, but he did not. Eventually he just walked to the pulpit and closed the meeting. Nobody ever said anything to me about not bearing my testimony, not even Elder Zollinger. I appreciated his willingness to let me work through this by myself. We were praying so many times each day I couldn't keep count, and we were fasting two meals about twice a week. I figured in time, my testimony would come.

A few days later, we rode our bikes further out into the country. It was a beautiful fall day and Elder Zollinger wanted to test his theory that out in rural areas people would be more likely to listen to us because they were not used to missionaries knocking on their doors. He was right. More people invited us inside their homes, but they still didn't want to know anything about our strange American church.

At one little cottage, situated on several acres, surrounded by apple and pear trees with ripe fruit, a very old man with white hair invited us in. His gardens and orchards were neat and well-maintained, but the inside of his cottage was the filthiest I had seen. I guessed the floor hadn't been mopped in years, probably because he didn't have a wife. Doing floors was women's work. He lived by himself. The dwelling was full of smells of things mildewed and rotten.

Still, we were glad to be invited in, instead of being sent down the road.

After taking our seats, the gentleman excused himself, saying he was going to fetch some refreshment. A moment later he handed us empty glasses that appeared every bit as dirty as his floor. Then he removed the cap from a tall green bottle that appeared just as grimy as the glasses. After wiping off the top of the bottle with a blackened and grimy palm, he poured our glasses full of clear, yellow *Sauft*, a brew he had made himself from his apples and pears.

Though we had been riding our bicycles in the warm sunshine, and were thirsty, we were not in any hurry to be poisoned. Elder Zollinger asked the man if he had any cakes or cookies to go with the drink. Cheerfully, the old man hurried to another room to find us something to munch on. My companion didn't waste any time pouring the contents of his glass into a wooden bucket. I hesitated.

"Doesn't it say in the *Bible* or *Book of Mormon* that the servants of the Lord cannot be harmed by poison?" I asked.

"Section eighty four of the *Doctrine & Covenants*. It says poison will not harm us, but it says nothing about shoring up our defenses against germs and filth."

The happy old man returned with some cookies on a plate. Not very many people had been kind to us. Not only had he invited us into his home, but he was sharing food and drink with us. The promise in the scriptures was good enough for me. I raised the glass to my lips, held my breath, and gulped down its contents.

I didn't hear very well as Elder Zollinger gave the screening discussion. I was listening to my stomach, wondering when the gurgling would start, wondering if I would be able to make it to the door before having to throw up. But none of those things happened. My stomach continued to feel fine. By the time Elder Zollinger finished the lesson, I was toying with the idea of asking for a refill, but I didn't.

While the man listened to the lesson and tried to answer some of the questions, it was soon evident he just wanted to be nice to us. He didn't know anything about our religion, and did not want to know more. We thanked him for his time, and for the refreshments, and headed down the street.

"For someone who does not *know* if the gospel is true, you demonstrated a lot of faith in there," Zollinger said.

"I know," I said, wondering if the word *know* was like the chain attached to the mean dog. Maybe I had already broken the chain holding me back, but didn't know it.

That evening I looked up the scripture in *Mark 16:18* which says the Lord's servants could not be harmed by poison:

. . .and if they drink any deadly thing, it shall not hurt them. . ..

I placed my hand on my stomach. No gurgling. I felt fine and slept good that night, as I always did.

SIX

One morning during our study together, Elder Zollinger had me copy down on two separate cards the names of all the books in the *Bible* and *Book of Mormon*. He said it would be easier for me to find scriptures if I knew the names and order of all the books in the scriptures. So now I had another memorization project.

Every morning as we left to go to work, the left pocket of my white shirt was crammed with green cards and folded up pages from the lesson plan. As we walked from house to house there was always a piece of paper in my hand. In addition to learning new words, I was constantly reviewing the words I had learned a day or a week previously.

I quickly realized there was a big difference between learning a word on a green card and being able to use it in the spontaneous flow of conversation. But I noticed as I took my turn giving the door approaches, and tried to converse with my companion and the many individuals we came in contact with every day, occasionally a word I had learned would slip into the conversation. Just a few at first, but more and more as time passed. As we read the scriptures every morning, my pronouncing errors gradually decreased. I was learning the language.

It took days for me to memorize the first two or three paragraphs of the screening discussion, but gradually I got better at it and learned the whole thing in about a month. The missionary lessons filled about a hundred single-spaced pages with very small type. It took me six weeks to learn the first lesson. I learned the second in less than four weeks. The next in about two weeks. My ability to memorize was improving by leaps and bounds. By the time I got to the sixth or last lesson, I memorized it in four days. I didn't consider myself exceptionally smart, I just got in a groove and worked really hard. I was constantly reviewing the lessons and vocabulary words so I would not forget and have to start all over again.

By the time I had learned all the lessons, I was so good at memorizing that I didn't want to stop. I bought a box in which I could store the little green cards in order, and began memorizing scriptures. First, I learned just the ones in our missionary discussions, then any ones that I liked or thought could be useful. We were reading scriptures about two hours every day, so I found many I liked, and began copying them on the green cards.

Upon memorizing a scripture I would number it and place it in the box. Then I would review the one immediately behind it, then skip one and review the one behind it, then skip two and review, skip four and review, skip eight and review, and so on. By the time I had five hundred cards in the box, I had to review a dozen or so every time I put in a new one. But I knew them all, verbatim, just like the lessons. Other missionaries began to look at me as a memorization genius. No. I had a system that worked, and I kept after it, every day.

Elder Zollinger finished his mission and returned to the

states. I worked with Elder Hillam for a few months, then went to Karlsruhe to work with Elder Wentz, the district leader. He had a car and I got to be the driver. That was great.

I didn't mind being a junior companion—less responsibility and more time for memorization. I still didn't *know* the church was true, but I knew the lessons as well as any missionary in the mission, and I had memorized more scriptures than anyone I had ever met. But Elder Kimball hadn't blessed me to know a thousand scriptures, but to help bring *a thousand souls* to a knowledge of the truth. That wasn't happening.

Sure, we were seeing a few baptisms, usually older women. It was only sixteen years since the end of World War II. Millions of German men did not come home after the war, leaving millions of war widows. Most of the women over forty were single and lonely. Some invited us in and were baptized. If there were thirty women in a church meeting, there might be three or four men. When we looked in on Catholic masses, it wasn't unusual for the congregation to be entirely made up of women, except maybe at Christmas and Easter.

I knew in order for Elder Kimball's blessing to be realized, major changes had to take place. But I had no idea what those changes might be. In addition to learning the lessons and scriptures, I was obeying all the rules, praying a dozen or so times every day, fasting once or twice a week, even getting up at five thirty every morning and doing fifty pushups. I didn't know what else to do. At this rate, tracting nearly sixty hours a week, instead of a thousand, I might see a dozen older women find the truth. And what was wrong with that? Nothing, except that Elder Kimball had blessed me to do something more.

That's when the zone leader came by for some business with my companion. I was sent out tracting with the zone leader's junior companion, Elder Roberts. At the first apartment building he asked me if I would like to know a little trick that would get us invited into twice as many homes. Of course, I wanted to know what he had in mind.

With a huge grin on his face, Elder Roberts slipped out of his suit coat, then put it on again, backwards. He turned his back to me so I could do up the buttons down the middle of his back. Then he knocked on the door. I had no idea what he was doing.

A middle-aged woman answered the door. He greeted her warmly, telling her he was a Lutheran minister. With the high black collar around the front of his neck, I guessed she believed him. Then nodding toward me he said he wanted her to meet a very nice young man from America who had a wonderful message about Jesus Christ. Could we come in so she could hear that message?

To my surprise, she invited us in and we gave her the screening discussion. When we were through she asked Elder Roberts if he was really a Lutheran minister. He confessed he was not, that he just wanted to have a little fun with her so she would let us in. She was not angry.

"I knew it from the start," she said. "You were too nice. Never met a Lutheran minister as nice as you." We all laughed, then made an appointment to come back and give her the first discussion.

As we walked up the stairs to the next apartment I asked Elder Roberts if he found it hard to lie, telling someone he was a Lutheran minister when indeed he was not. He responded by asking me if I found it hard, showing someone a picture of the Swiss temple and then telling them I was conducting a survey. I reached out and rang the next doorbell.

We gave four screening discussions that morning, and made two appointments for first discussions, probably the most successful three hours of tracting I had ever experienced. We had only one door slammed in our faces.

In an apartment building we had rung the bell twice when we noticed movement in the tiny peek hole in the middle of the door. Someone was looking at us from the inside, and was choosing not to open the door. This happened a lot. To my amazement, Elder Roberts had a response.

A few minutes later we returned to that same door. Elder Roberts pulled a cigarette lighter out of his pocket. Holding the flame in front of the magnifying glass in the peek hole, he rang the bell, then shouted *"Feuer!"* A few seconds later the door flew open. Instead of seeing the entry hall on fire, the poor woman saw two grinning young missionaries. Before we could give her the door approach she slammed the door as hard as she could, right in our faces. Still, we had had a good morning. We got in the car and drove to a favorite restaurant to have our lunch.

We were discussing our morning adventures over two deep-fried chunks of *Wienerschnitzel* when Elder Roberts asked if I was ever tempted to stare at beautiful women. I confessed I was only human, then noticed that he was looking at two nuns seated several tables away. They had removed their white hats, and even though their hair was cropped short without any styling, they were two of the most beautiful women I had ever seen. One was tall and blond with deep blue eyes and a smartly shaped nose. She could have been a model in any American fashion magazine. The other one had brown hair with a natural wave that curled under at the nape of her neck. Her complexion was the smoothest I had ever seen, and she had green eyes that reminded me of Emerald Lake at the top of Mt. Timpanogos.

"Are they really that attractive, or have we just been in the mission field too long?" Elder Roberts asked.

"I can't answer that," I said. "But they probably have furry armpits and long black hair on their legs."

My comment didn't register with him.

"I want a picture," he said.

"It's not polite to take pictures of the natives," I said.

"I want *my* picture taken with *them*," he explained, "but I don't want one of those cheese shots." He asked me to go to the car, which was parked at the curb just outside the front door of the restaurant, and get his camera out of a bag in the back seat, then go to the front of the car and lean nonchalantly against the hood. It would be an outside photo, so we agreed on the *f* stop and shutter speed settings. I knew how to make the adjustments.

"Be ready to shoot when they come out the front door," he said. "But don't do it until I step between them and take each one by the hand. That's the picture I want."

"Holding hands with nuns?" I questioned. "There has to be a mission rule against that."

"I'm not going to hug them, just hold their hands, like a

quick handshake. Nothing wrong with that. Might get slapped, but on the other hand we might get in a conversation with them—help them join the church, move to Utah, marry returned missionaries and have ten kids. We will be eternally blessed for making it all possible."

Reluctantly, I agreed to his insane plan. I went out to the car to get ready with the camera while he paid for the meal. I was toying with the focus adjustment when the two nuns emerged from the restaurant, stopping in the bright sunshine to adjust their white headdresses. I raised the camera to my eye. They didn't seem to notice me.

Through the view finder I could see Elder Roberts coming from the restaurant, directly behind the nuns, a bright smile on his face. He had to wait a second or two as the two women finished adjusting their headgear, but as soon as their hands dropped to their sides, the bold missionary slipped between them, grinning toward the camera as he took hold of two white, feminine hands. I snapped the picture, then quickly turned the knob so I could take a second shot. By the time I did that, the nuns were looking at Elder Roberts, surprised looks on their young faces, trying to pull their hands away.

As I walked up to join the curious threesome, Elder Roberts was graciously thanking them for letting him have his picture taken with them. He explained that he was going to send the photo to his friends in Utah who would be amazed at the beauty of the nuns in Germany. At this point I was wondering if we could count our time with the nuns as missionary work, or if something else was going on.

Noticing my approach, the one with the deep emerald

eyes asked where I was from. When I told her California, they both started asking questions about Hollywood and Disneyland. I had never been to Hollywood, and to Disneyland only once, but I answered their questions like an expert.

We introduced ourselves. They told us their names. The tall one was *Schwester* Maria and emerald eyes called herself *Schwester* Frieda. We learned they weren't real nuns, but nuns in training. If they behaved themselves, they would be fully initiated into their order in a few years. Maria was twenty one, and Frieda was twenty, just like me. We chatted for a while, shook hands, said good-bye, then talked some more. After a while we shook hands again, said good-bye again, then talked some more. They didn't seem to want to leave any more than we did. Finally, after showing them the pictures in our *Black Book*, we gave each of them a *Book of Mormon* in which we had written personal notes about how wonderful it was to meet them. Then we got in our car and drove away.

My heart was pounding, my palms sweating, and I knew it wasn't the spirit moving me in the work of the Lord. Just when I thought I had everything under control, the weakness of the flesh had never felt so good.

That night as we reported seven screening discussions and three first lesson appointments to our companions, the zone leader looked at Elder Roberts.

"No unusual adventures for me to explain to the mission president?"

"Nope," Elder Roberts responded, cheerily.

"No pretending to be Catholic priests, or holding lighters

in front of peek holes?"

Elder Roberts looked away. Apparently he had been in trouble before. Perhaps that was why he was being kept under close supervision by a zone leader. I decided to rescue him.

"We took pictures of some very unusual nuns," I said.

"Anything I need to report to the president?" he asked.

"Of course not."

"Good."

The zone leader and Elder Roberts put on their coats, shook hands with us, and headed for the door. But before they left, I made Elder Roberts promise to send me one of the nun pictures. He said he would, then winked at me as he disappeared through the door.

It had been a long and eventful day. Ten minutes later, after saying our prayers, we turned out the lights and went to bed. But for the first time since coming to Germany, I didn't go to sleep immediately. At first I just pondered the events of what I was certain was my most enjoyable day in the mission field. We had talked to a lot of people, had plenty of success, and had more fun than I thought was possible for missionaries to have, without technically breaking the rules. There were no rules against imitating Lutheran ministers and igniting cigarette lighters in front of peek holes. Then there was the photo session with the nuns.

Under the covers, in the dark, eyes closed, I could still see that beautiful face and those emerald eyes smiling kindly down upon me. Once again my heart was pounding and my palms were sweating. Then I felt guilty, repeatedly telling myself I hadn't done anything wrong.

But I knew I had no business feeling this way. I was a missionary. I felt ashamed, and hoped I wouldn't have to confess to Elder Wentz or President Gardner.

I had to admit to myself that I wasn't as righteous and spiritual as I formerly thought. It didn't matter that I knew every word in every sentence in every paragraph of the discussions, and had five hundred verses of scripture on the tip of my tongue. I still didn't *know*, and because of that flaw, I was probably more vulnerable to the temptations of the flesh than other missionaries were. I would have to be very, very careful. With these thoughts and feelings thundering in my head and heart, I finally fell into an exhausted slumber an hour or two before the sun came up.

SEVEN

The next morning I told Elder Wentz I was determined to overcome the temptations of the flesh by ceasing to acknowledge the existence of beautiful women. He was propped up on one elbow in his bed, his favorite position for breakfast, eating peeled oranges and sliced liverwurst, possibly his favorite breakfast meal. I told him he had my permission to slug me in the shoulder or demand payment of a *Duestche Mark* if he caught me staring at an attractive woman. It didn't matter that Germany was the miniskirt capitol of Europe. I was determined to not look at them. Whenever a young woman would enter my field of vision, I would turn my head the other way. He happily agreed, making his right hand into a fist, and slapping it against the open palm of his left hand. It was obvious he could hardly wait to apply bruises to my bony shoulders.

He slugged me three times that first day, two times the next, but never again after that. After about three days I simply didn't notice miniskirts or the women who wore them anymore. As long as a certain nun didn't stumble across my path, I figured I was well on my way to being totally immune to the temptations of the flesh.

I knew I was succeeding the day I was driving through Karlsruhe in a rainstorm. We were late for an appointment, or hurrying to the church. I don't remember which. I had just whizzed around a sharp corner when Elder Wentz asked me if I knew what I had just done.

"No, what?"

He said I had just driven through a puddle and drenched the prettiest yellow miniskirt he had ever seen, and the girl wearing it wasn't bad either, apparently standing on the corner waiting for a bus. I could honestly say I hadn't noticed her, but I was still sorry I had gotten her wet.

Several nights later as we were getting ready for bed, I told Elder Wentz that I didn't want to be a missionary any more, not if I couldn't know if the things I was teaching were true. It was simply too hard, too much work, requiring too much sacrifice. If I could not do it right, if I couldn't know it was true, then I just didn't want to do it anymore. If God didn't care enough about me to give me a testimony, then I didn't care enough about his work to keep doing it.

I had dropped a bombshell, and half expected Elder Wentz to run to the phone and call the mission president. Or at least preach a sermon and bear some testimony. Instead, he simply extended his right hand toward the little table between us. He pressed the side of his little finger against the surface of the table, applying an increasing amount of pressure until there was a loud pop. Then he pushed the next finger against the table until it popped. Then the middle finger, the forefinger, even the thumb. When all the fingers on his right hand had popped, he extended his left hand and popped each of those fingers. But he wasn't through. He started again with the right hand, and it wasn't until he had popped all ten fingers three times that he looked up at me.

"What are you going to do, Elder Nelson?"

"I fast two meals two or three times a week, like we are supposed to do," I said, "but nothing spiritual ever happens. You know how hard I study and work. I don't know what else to do."

"Maybe you need to fast more than two meals."

"It's against the rules."

"That rule is made for the weakest of the weak, elders like me who might pass out or faint. Not for the ones like you who jump out of bed at five thirty and do fifty pushups, then run up and down stairs, two at a time all day with hormones oozing out of every pour. It wouldn't hurt you to fast a week."

"You're kidding."

"No. You need to show the Lord you are ready. And I think now is the time."

Nothing more needed to be said. My fast had begun. Every time I awakened during the night, I rolled out of bed onto my knees and pleaded my case to God. I begged him to pour his spirit on me so I could know the truth of the things I was teaching. When my knees hurt so bad and I was shivering so much from the cold that I could hardly concentrate, I would crawl back under the covers, sleep a little, then roll onto my knees once again. I began to wonder if there was any God at all. He surely didn't seem to want to answer my prayers.

The next day I skipped all three meals. We had our usual work to do, but Elder Wentz left me pretty much to myself. When we were around other missionaries or investigators I tried to be normal and cheerful, and generally not give any hints about what I was doing. Elder Wentz respected my privacy. As far as I know he didn't say anything to anyone.

The second night was a lot harder than the first. It was harder to get out of bed. Whenever I did, the cold made my teeth chatter. The heavens remained closed. I would feel angry, then so very sad. Sometimes I wanted to cry, but would not allow it.

I didn't use any of this time to review lessons or vocabulary. I focused my attention on the scriptures, the ones I had learned. And I read favorite parts of the *Bible* and *Book of Mormon*. As time passed I was spending most of my study time in III Nephi and the four gospels of the *New Testament*, the passages about Jesus. It became more and more apparent that the testimony I needed concerned Jesus and his mission. Everything else would take care of itself. I read about his birth, his sermons, his teachings, his miracles, his death, and the resurrection. The more I studied, the more I needed to continue. I began to crave the words of Jesus as much as I craved food and drink.

That second day I began to feel dizzy. My companion persuaded me to drink some apple cider. Wow. It surged into my system like a shot of adrenaline. The dizziness disappeared. By this time I was walking like a zombie—no two stairs at a time. Frequently I had to shake my head to clear my vision, especially when I was reading. Elder Wentz continued to go quietly about his business, leaving me almost entirely to myself.

I kind of thought that if the Lord wanted to answer my prayers and give me a testimony, I would hear a voice. I was listening all the time, but no voice came. Sometime in the middle of the third night, after another episode of pleading and begging on my knees, I crawled back into bed, where I waited for a long time. Eventually my stomach stopped growling, and I felt almost too weak to breathe.

Suddenly, a warm tingly feeling, like a gentle ocean wave, washed over my head and face, then down the entire length of my body clear to my toes, gradually increasing in strength, like tiny hot hands lovingly squeezing every cell in my body. My heart was pounding like it was about to burst, and the tears were streaming off my cheeks onto the pillow.

Though my eyes were closed, I thought I could see the bearded face of the man I had been reading about. The image was brief, fuzzy, and far away. I don't know how long it took for all this to occur, but when the feeling finally faded, I was too exhausted to raise my head, too tired to wake up Elder Wentz and tell him what had happened. Almost before I knew it, I fell into a deep, peaceful sleep.

The next morning I rolled out of bed and announced that the fast was over. Elder Wentz asked if my prayers had been answered. I said they had. He wanted to know more. I reached for my *Bible*, vaguely remembering a verse I had read several months back. The prophet Jeremiah had described an experience similar to mine. I found it in *Jeremiah 20:9*, and read it out loud:

> *Then I said I will not make mention of him, nor speak any more in his name. But his word was in mine heart as a burning fire shut up in my bones, and I was weary with forbearing, and I could not stay.*

I explained what had happened during the night. I knew my philosophy professor might argue that my experience was more emotional than spiritual, but I *knew* what had happened. I *knew* my prayers had been answered, and I *knew* Jesus was my savior, and everybody else's too, and that I had been called by him to take that message to the world, and I intended to do just that.

The following Monday I received a letter from President Gardner promoting me to senior companion, in Reutlingen, a city of about ninety thousand, not far from Stuttgart. I was to leave immediately. With the language, lessons and scriptures in my head, and a testimony in my heart, it was time to roll up my sleeves and find those *thousand souls*.

EIGHT

Upon arriving in Reutlingen I met my new companion, Elder Egli, fresh from Salt Lake City. He quickly explained that due to some childhood illnesses, he hadn't grown up with normal physical activity. He hadn't learned to ride a bike until a few weeks before his mission. He was an honor student in school, so he probably wouldn't have any trouble learning the language and lessons, but riding a bike on narrow streets at rush hour would definitely be a problem. I figured running up and down the stairs, two at a time, in high rise apartment buildings might be a challenge too.

The next morning at five thirty I invited Elder Egli to do pushups with me. He said he thought he had signed up for missionary service, not basic training in the military. I liked his sense of humor. I'm not sure he liked mine. I didn't have any. I was too intent on baptizing *a thousand souls*.

When I asked him if I needed to adjust our schedule because of his physical limitations, he said I should do what I normally did, and he would do his best to keep up. He was a good sport. So that's the way it was.

The second day, he rode his bike into a curb, resulting in a horrible end-over-end crash. I was relieved that he was still alive, but figured we were done for the day and would have to return to our apartment. Elder Egli had other ideas. He brushed the dirt and gravel from his hands, tucked the torn part of his coat into the torn hole, shoved his broken glasses in his pocket, then nodded for me to lead the way. We finished a full day of tracting, but he was still limping as he struggled up the steps to our apartment that night. There were other bike crashes in the weeks to come, but none as serious as the first.

What Elder Egli might have lacked in physical coordination and stamina, he made up for in intellectual capacity. He was able to memorize vocabulary words, lessons and scriptures faster than anyone I had ever known, except perhaps Elders Heiner and Hughes whom everyone thought held the mission record, having memorized the six discussions in about five weeks. Nevertheless, Elder Egli was able to memorize at least twice as fast as I had been able to do it. I think he had a photographic memory. But best of all I liked his attitude. Whatever I wanted to do, he would try, regardless of the potential suffering and injury to his body. He never complained.

Within a few weeks we were tracting more hours and giving more screening discussions than any pair of elders or sisters in the mission. Elder Egli was doing pushups with me in the morning, though still a long way from my standard fifty. He could go to the top of a five-story apartment two steps at a time without stopping, whip out his *Black Book*, ask the survey questions, and once in a while get in for a screening discussion. I was so proud of his progress.

Within a month we had people preparing for baptism; a single woman, and a couple with a nine-year-old daughter. The mother and daughter seemed determined to go all the way. They read in the *Book of Mormon* every day. But after a few lessons the father started avoiding us. I don't think he wanted to give up his smoking, and by then he knew about tithing. The wife was pestering him to listen to us, and he was resisting.

Then one day he came in and sat down with us. I was sure the wife had been applying pressure behind our backs. He didn't want to be there, but he was, and he told us he knew enough English that we didn't have to give the lessons in German if we didn't want to. I asked him where he had learned English. He was not the studious type.

He said he used to work at a U.S. Army base where the soldiers spent a lot of time teaching him to say things in English. There was a twinkle in his eye. He was having too much fun telling us this. He was setting us up for I knew not what. He asked if I would like to hear what the soldiers taught him. I nodded that I would.

He cut loose with more versions of the F word than I had heard in gym class and Marine Corps basic training combined. The whole time his wife was grinning, so happy her reluctant husband was able to converse in English with the missionaries. She had no idea what he was saying. He continued with his monologue, repeating with a strong German accent every filthy word or phrase known to the American military. Then he got up and left the house, laughing all the way. The wife and daughter were baptized a few weeks later, but not the husband. The other woman was also baptized. I figured that if the mission president would leave Elder Egli and me together for a year, we would probably baptize thirty or forty people, and that would be some kind of record, a rate at which I could reach Elder Kimball's goal in about fifty years.

People who have not been on missions might get the idea that tracting is fun and easy. On the contrary, it is the hardest work I have ever done. It was such a wonderful relief to have a day off for a baptism or a mission conference. Even going to stake conference or church meetings was a wonderful change of pace.

And sometimes those meetings provided some excellent entertainment, like the time we were attending stake conference in Stuttgart. Apostle Ezra Taft Benson was speaking through an interpreter, explaining the scripture in the *Doctrine & Covenants* that says, "Many are called but few are and chosen." But instead of quoting the verse verbatim, he made an attempt at humor by creating a pun. He said, "Many are cold but few are frozen."

The interpreter paused. The missionaries could appreciate his dilemma. How do you translate something like that so the comment would still be funny? Elder Benson waited patiently for the interpreter to figure out what to say.

"I cannot translate Elder Benson's last comment, without losing the intended humor," the interpreter finally said, in German. "But it was very funny, so would everyone please laugh." The audience roared, and I'm sure Elder Benson was wondering why the German people found a simple little pun so funny.

Another time I was attending a sacrament meeting in Esslingen, a little town not far from Reutlingen, listening to a lengthy sermon by one of the newer missionaries. His command of the language was passable, barely.

The elder described an incident growing up in which his

father had spanked him with a stick. The word for stick is *stock*. The word for tail is *Schwanz*. I don't know how the elder mixed up these two words, but he said his father used to beat him with his *Schwanz*, or tail. What the elder didn't know was that in German slang, or gutter language, *Schwanz* also means penis.

Of course the congregation roared. This was very funny. The elder paused, realizing he had made a mistake—used the wrong word. Suddenly he realized what he thought he had said wrong. He remembered that *Schwanz* meant tail. So he apologized for his mistake, saying his father didn't have a *Schwanz*.

The Lord's spirit departed from the meetinghouse. The bewildered missionary couldn't understand why people were laughing so hard, tears streaming down their cheeks. The red-faced bishop and his two counselors were leaning forward, faces in their palms, trying to hide their uncontrollable mirth. It was a good thing the sacrament portion of the meeting was over, and it was a good thing no investigators were present.

On another occasion we noticed fliers posted on telephone poles and bulletin boards in our tracting area announcing a lecture by a Catholic cleric on the evils of Mormonism. As we entertained the possibility of attending the meeting, it occurred to us that we might go in disguise, thinking the cleric might be more likely to libel himself if he thought there were no Mormons present to catch him in his lies. And if he didn't know Mormons were present, the possibility of a confrontation would be removed.

But as I thought about it I remembered an incident at the

end of basic training in the Marine Corps where I attempted to become invisible in order to avoid a confrontation over my religious beliefs. At the time I had vowed with myself never to do that again.

It was the last day of basic training. A celebration was announced for those of us who had survived by not dropping out. It was a scorching hot August afternoon in Virginia. We were assembled in a large hall, seated in long rows behind tables, about two hundred and fifty of us. There was no air conditioning.

For the first time since joining the Marine Corps, we were allowed to sing the Marine Corps hymn. We had proven our worthiness by enduring to the end.

After singing the hymn a few times and listening to some brief congratulatory remarks by some of the officers, it was announced we were going to have a party. The back doors flew open and men pushing hand trucks stacked high with beer and pop entered the room. The cases of beverage were slid down the tables for distribution to the men. There was plenty, more than we could consume in several hours.

I grabbed a couple of 7-ups and joined the celebration. After half an hour some of the men were feeling pretty good, including the officers and sergeants who were drinking with us. Finally, one of the sergeants went to the podium at the front of the room and yelled into the microphone for us to give him our full attention.

He said he had noticed that some of the men were not drinking beer.

"Marines are men, and men drink beer," he announced, like he was revealing one of the foundation truths of the universe. Then he ordered all of us who had not been drinking beer to do so now. Looking around the hall, it appeared that about a dozen of the men were not drinking the beer.

Some of the men were not obeying the new order. I certainly wasn't, but with over two hundred and fifty men in the room, I didn't think they noticed my abstinence.

Seeing possible resistance to the new order, groups of officers marched down the middle aisle. Then beginning at the back row, they began singling out men whom they suspected of not drinking. If the object of their attention refused to raise a can of beer to his lips and swallow, they quickly gathered around that individual, shouting, yelling, cursing, giving them all the usual harassment we had been enduring for six weeks. Most of their targets gave in at this point and started drinking. Those who did not were subjected to a new kind of harassment. One officer would begin pouring a can of beer on the victim's head and shoulders. Then a second officer would join in, then a third, and so on until the drenched recruit finally gave in and started drinking.

The officers were a hundred percent successful in getting their subjects to drink, and would soon be at my table. I had no intention of drinking. I was more angry than I was scared. They had overstepped their bounds. They had no right to do this. Already in my head I was composing a letter of complaint to my congressman. But I didn't want to be showered in beer, either.

I picked up an empty beer can, washed it out with 7-Up, then poured it about a third full of the soda. When the officers surrounded me and gave the order to drink, I simply smiled, raised the beer can containing 7-Up to my lips, and gulped down the entire contents. Some of the officers exchanged glances, as if they suspected something might be fishy. I had been too easy. They knew I was a Mormon. But they were drunk and not thinking clearly, so they moved to the next nondrinker. I had fooled them. My companions congratulated me for being so clever.

Finally, the officers were circled around the last man in the room they suspected of not drinking beer. We were in the same platoon, but I don't remember his name, only that he was from Minnesota, a tall, blond good-looking fellow. During basic he had attended church on Sundays, but he was not Mormon.

He told the officers it was against his religious beliefs to drink beer, and he would not do it. The first officer began pouring beer over his head, then the second, the third, the fourth. They filled his pockets, even his shoes with what looked like yellow urine. He was drenched from head to foot, but had not swallowed a single drop. He reminded me of Joseph Smith defying the guards at Liberty Jail. Suddenly, I realized that while my behavior had been practical and convenient, his behavior was noble and valiant.

I was about ready to hurry forward to stand beside my friend, telling the officers that 7-Up was in my can, that I had not consumed a single drop of beer, and they could not make me do it, either. But it was too late. A sober, higher-ranking officer entered the room and quickly put an end to what was going on.

I told Elder Egli it was my conviction after that experience that the right thing to do, if we went to the lecture about the Mormons, was to march right up to the front row and sit where everyone could see us.

We learned from Elder Ludke, our district leader, that the man giving the lecture was Heinrich Hermann, the golden boy of the Catholic priesthood. He was a priest now, but would probably be a bishop before thirty, and probably someday be a cardinal. With youth and luck on his side he might even be the pope someday. Ludke said he had read an article about the young priest, that everywhere he went, the attendance at the churches increased over fifty percent in a few months.

The night for the lecture finally arrived. Not only did we march in fifteen minutes early and find places on the front row, but we hauled in a huge tape recorder with a microphone and set it up in front of the podium. If *Pfarr* Hermann was planning on libeling the Mormon Church, we figured it would be nice for him to know that every word was being recorded.

The auditorium had a four-hundred seat capacity. It was already about half full, and people were still streaming in. It appeared there would be a capacity audience. The big question in my head was why so many people were coming to a lecture about the Mormons. Based on the response to our tracting visits, the people of Reutlingen didn't seem that curious to know more about us. Perhaps they just wanted to attend a lecture by the Catholic golden boy, regardless of subject.

When it was time for the meeting to begin, *Pfarr* Hermann entered from the rear. A murmur passed through the audience as people turned to watch him stride down the aisle. He was a handsome man, his hair golden and wavy with an uncombed look. He moved with strength and confidence, agile and firm, like a star athlete. Electricity passed through the air, and there was a tingling in the back of my neck. I guessed this was how people felt in the congregations of Nauvoo when Joseph Smith entered the room. I wasn't surprised that there were a lot more women than men in the audience.

After shaking hands with people along the aisle, Hermann leaped up the stairs to the stage, two at a time, then took a seat behind the podium. A lesser priest, a mere mouse of a man, said a prayer. His words were abstract and stiff, with no feeling—at least not for me. Then six boys, dressed in black and white robes, sang a song so difficult and complex that I never could figure out the melody, if there was one.

Then the priest who had said the prayer returned to the pulpit, where he stared nervously at our big tape recorder. He thanked *Pharr* Hermann for driving down from Stuttgart to help fortify the people of Reutlingen against the Mormon invasion. This comment caught us by surprise, causing us to wonder if our work was having a larger impact in this community than we realized. We were visiting hundreds of homes, giving dozens of screening discussions, teaching gospel discussions, and in recent weeks had even experienced a few baptisms. With great difficulty, and much effort, the work was moving ahead, and now we knew the Catholics were getting worried. It felt great knowing Catholic priests were lying awake at nights worrying about us college students from America who hardly knew the language, and had no formal training as ministers.

After the introduction, *Pfarr* Hermann moved quietly to the pulpit. After spreading out his various notes and books across the flat surface in front of him, he looked down at us and our tape recorder. He didn't look nervous and worried, like the other priest. Instead, he smiled at us.

"I'd like to thank the young Americans for coming to our meeting tonight," he said, "to be our visual aids, to give us something concrete to look at and ponder as we learn of old Lucifer's plan to undermine two thousand years of holy Catholic tradition." Some of the people said *Ahmen* while others clapped.

"Now, if I were Lucifer," the priest continued, his voice growing louder, more confident, "and I wanted to send out messengers to deceive the people of God, I would not send contentious old priests with gray hair, bulging bellies and wrinkled faces. The people of God would be frightened by such men, and not let them in their homes. No, I would send handsome young men with freshly-scrubbed faces—inno-cent-looking, like Adam in the Garden of Eden. It wouldn't matter that they were too young to know foreign languages and had no formal training. People would not fear them, and would therefore be open to their deceits and manipulations." Some of the people looked at us and hissed.

"Now, if I were a Mormon bishop or apostle, and lived in the valley of the Great Salt Lake, and had only three or four wives in my harem, and wanted a lot more, where would I look? Where might there be lots of attractive, unattached women? Germany, of course. Five million of our men were killed in the war, leaving millions of women without husbands. Lonely and for the most part destitute, Germany's women are the ripe fruit the Mormons had come to harvest.

"Now those bishops and apostles are smart enough not to come themselves. With long gray beards, and overfed bellies hanging out so far they cannot see their feet, the Mormon leaders know it would be foolish to come themselves, for surely they would frighten all the German women away." Hermann paused so everyone but us could laugh.

"So they send over their handsome young men, scrubbed faces and boiling over with youth and zest—without training and knowledge, so they seem innocent and harmless. First they teach, then they baptize, then they send their victims back to Utah to fill the empty harems of the less capable Mormon leaders who are not wealthy or capable enough to attract plural wives on their own. And while all this is going on, Lucifer and his hosts are celebrating." Again some booing.

"Do you agree with what I say?" Hermann asked, looking down at me and my companion. We were caught totally off guard. We didn't think he would speak to us. Of course we didn't agree with what he was saying, but neither were we prepared to participate in the meeting.

"Do you agree with what I say?" he asked a second time. It was obvious he wanted us to respond, but it wasn't appropriate to give him the screening discussion, any more than to ask him the survey questions. Slowly I stood up, desperately praying that words would come to me, any words, hopefully German words.

"My father had only one wife," I said. Everyone was

listening, no heckling. I continued.

"My grandfathers had only one wife each. Every bishop I have ever known had only one wife. In fact I have lived in Utah and California my entire life, and can honestly say I have never met a Mormon who had more than one wife. Sure, the Mormons used to have plural wives, as did Abraham, Isaac and Jacob, even David and Solomon, but they don't do it anymore. I don't think the Jews practice polygamy any more, and neither do the Mormons." Then I turned away from the audience to face *Pfarr* Hermann. My tongue was loosed. The words were coming more easily now.

"Someone gave you bad information about the Mormons wanting plural wives. About all I can say is shame on those who would tell such lies." To my amazement some of the people in the audience cheered. I was wishing we could get their names so we could teach them the first lesson.

"It is well known that the Mormons claim to have a gold bible," Hermann said, trying to regain control of the audience. "The first Mormon, Joe Smith, walked into the woods one day and found a bible made of solid gold. He brought it home and called it *The Book of Mormon*. He must have been a pretty strong boy to carry a bible made of solid gold." He paused so the audience could laugh. I looked at the tape recorder to make sure it was running.

When I looked back up at *Pfarr* Hermann, he was looking directly back at me. I could see beads of sweat on his forehead. It didn't surprise me that telling lies about sacred things could cause a man to sweat.

"Perhaps the young man who set us straight on polygamy would like to give us his version of the gold bible story."

I could hardly believe he was giving me an opportunity to speak again. I wanted to kick myself for coming to something like this so ill-prepared. Never again. He nodded for me to come up to the pulpit. I picked up the briefcase that contained my scriptures and climbed onto the stage. When I stepped to the pulpit, Hermann moved a little to one side instead of sitting down. I suppose he wanted to be close to me so he could take over should things get out of hand.

Slowly I opened my *Bible* to *John* 10:16. I didn't need to read it because I knew it by heart:

> *And other sheep I have, which are not of this fold. . . and they shall hear my voice; and there shall be one fold and one shepherd.*

I told them how after the resurrection Jesus visited the people of ancient America; how the religious leaders of those people wrote down the things he said, along with descriptions of many religious and historical events. Instead of writing their history on animal skins and paper which could perish in the elements, or copper which corrodes, or brass whose hard surface makes writing difficult, the people wrote their history on gold which by nature is a very soft metal and can be pounded into very thin sheets which are easy to write upon. At that time gold was plentiful in America, so why not use it to record important events?

I told them how an angel of the Lord in 1820 led a young man named Joseph Smith to this ancient record, then how Joseph Smith, with the power of God, translated and published it as the *Book of Mormon*, named after one of the ancient prophets who helped prepare the record. I said the *Book of Mormon* did not replace the *Bible*, but was another book like the *Bible*, a second witness of the divinity of Jesus Christ.

While the audience seemed very respectful, listening to every word, *Pfarr* Hermann was fidgeting, obviously trying to figure out a way to get rid of me. I knew my minutes were numbered.

I bent over, picked up my briefcase with both hands, as if it were very heavy and eased it onto the top of the pulpit, as if it were full of bricks, golden bricks. I had everyone's attention, even *Pfarr* Hermann's.

"Do any of you really think the leaders of the Mormon Church would tell the whole world how our book came from golden plates without being able to back up such a claim? Do you think young men like me and my companion would come all the way to Germany, at considerable cost, if we didn't know the golden plate story was true?"

I opened the briefcase, just a little, and peeked in.

"Who would like to see what's in my briefcase?" I asked. Most of the hands went up.

"If I pull out a gold plate and let all of you look at it, how many of you will agree to be baptized next week?" No hands went up.

"If I let *Pfarr* Hermann take a gold plate to the university at Tübingen, and the archeologists there determine that the writing on it is indeed the writing of ancient peoples, then how many of you will agree to give up your alcohol and tobacco, and pay tithing to the Mormon Church?" Again, no hands went up, and I waited for what seemed a long time.

I pulled my briefcase from the podium, returning it to the floor by my feet.

"You see, one does not come to know the things of God by looking at golden plates or other scientific evidence. So I am not going to show you what is in my briefcase." There were some murmurs of disappointment.

"The things of God can only be known by the Spirit of God."

I read them the promise in Moroni 10:4-5. Then I told them a condensed version of my struggle to know the truth of these things, my fasting and praying, then closed, quoting from Jeremiah 20:9:

But his word was in mine heart, as a burning fire shut up in my bones. . ..

Again, I didn't have to read it because I knew it by heart. I stepped to one side, thanking *Pfarr* Hermann for letting me explain our message.

His closing remarks were sober and sincere. He said we were nice young men. He urged the people to treat us with kindness, but to remember who they were and what the Catholic church had done for them and their ancestors through a hundred generations.

As we hauled our huge tape recorder out of the meeting hall, I couldn't help but wonder if our reception in Reutlingen would be any different now. How many of these people, if any, would invite us into their homes to hear our message? I hoped there would be many. We would find out soon enough.

As we prepared our weekly reports for mission headquarters that night, we described the meeting with *Pfarr* Hermann, and how wonderful it had been to be permitted to preach our message to hundreds of potential investigators, all at once.

A few days later I received a special delivery letter from the mission home, transferring me to Stuttgart where I was to become the district leader.

NINE

It was hard leaving Reutlingen just when it appeared the work was beginning to make great forward strides, but on the other hand, Stuttgart was the largest city in the mission, with hundreds of thousands of potential converts. Stuttgart was home of the Stuttgart Stake, and boasted a chapel as nice as the newer ones in Utah. There were lots of active members to mingle with our prospective converts. As district leader my sphere of influence would broaden to include the labors of ten missionaries, instead of two. Perhaps this was where Elder Kimball's blessing would find fulfillment. Perhaps Stuttgart housed the thousand souls I would help find the truth.

But I knew that even ten elders tracting all day, every day, would not bring it about. There had to be a better way, and after the meeting with *Pfarr* Hermann in Reutlingen, I wondered if group meetings like that might be the better way. If we could be like that handsome Catholic and bring hundreds of people together in auditoriums, people who came because they were curious about the Mormons, then wonderful things might happen. The words of Paul to the Roman saints, one of my memorized scriptures, kept coming into my mind:

So then faith cometh by hearing, and hearing by

the word of God. Romans 10:17

People could hear a lot more of the word of God in a gathering like the one in Reutlingen than two elders coming to their door asking survey questions. Plus I liked the idea of interested people coming to us rather than our having to tract out anyone and everyone at random. But all this would have to wait, at least until I was more familiar with district leader duties. I was determined to make the district a well-oiled machine with all the elders working hard, doing everything they were supposed to be doing so we would be blessed in our labors. Almost every day my new companion, Elder Burke, and I were working with different pairs of elders, making sure they were tracting as effectively as possible and giving lots of screening discussions.

I enjoyed working with and getting to know the missionaries in the district, especially the more serious ones, like Elders Krueger and Boundy. One day as we were riding a bus to a tracting area (our companions were using the car), Elder Krueger told me about his patriarchal blessing, like it was one of the most important things in his life, giving him direction and purpose that he wouldn't have had otherwise. I don't remember any of the specifics, only how his words made me feel.

I was active in the church as a teenager, but whenever the leaders encouraged us to make appointments to receive patriarchal blessings, I never did it. I just never felt a need or an urgency to do it. But I did now. I was moved deeply by Elder Krueger's thoughts about his blessing, so much so that I wrote to President Gardner asking for permission to get my own patriarchal blessing. Permission was granted. An appointment was made.

A few weeks later, early on a spring morning, my companion and I got on the train and traveled to Heilbron, the home of Patriarch Emil Geist. From the train window the German countryside had never looked more lush and beautiful. I never tired of looking at the little German farms with their stone walls, animals, wagons, barns and homes.

It was a short walk from the station to the Geist home. He lived in an older section of town which had been missed by the American bombers in World War II. It was a small home with neatly-painted shutters, and a perfect yard and garden. I had never met Patriarch Geist before, but I had seen him at stake conferences in Stuttgart. He was a short man, with snow-white hair, probably in his mid-seventies.

After a brief greeting I was ushered into the room to the left of the front door where he gave the blessings, a home office of sorts, full of what I thought were ancient tapestries and antique furniture. He motioned for me to be seated in a comfortable chair in the middle of the room.

Looking up I noticed the ceiling was painted bright red, in stark contrast to the beige and brown colors surrounding me. I remember wanting to ask him why he painted the ceiling red. I didn't think it had anything to do with the spiritual nature of what happened in the room. On the other hand, I wondered if perhaps the spirit became more active when it descended through a bright red ceiling, but I doubted it.

Normally, from what I've observed in the church, patriarchs like to get acquainted with their subjects before giving blessings; discuss interests, background, goals, etc. Such was not the case with *Bruder* Geist. He didn't know that in college my major was physics, that I intended to become an engineer, that I hated English classes but loved to read. My dislike for English classes began in high school when a friend and I decided to switch names on essays we were handing in. I had told my friend that he always got A's on his assignments because the teacher liked him, and that I always got C's because the teacher didn't like me. He didn't agree, thinking he received A's because he was a better writer. I convinced him that by switching names on the essays being turned in, we could test my theory, so we did it. When the papers were returned, my paper with his name on it got the A, and his paper with my name on it got the C. Thus I convinced my friend that in this class, at least, grades were based more on personal preference than accomplishment or skill. I liked math and science classes because it didn't matter if the teacher liked you or not; if you got all the problems right you got an A. In college my interests continued to gravitate toward the sciences. At the time I left on my mission, my major was physics. I intended to become an engineer. Nobody told any of this to Patriarch Geist.

Standing behind me, he simply put his old but firm hands on my head and started to bless me, in German. It was one of the longest patriarchal blessings I have known to be given. After a few minutes a strange pattern began to develop as he made promises concerning my ability with words. He said the Lord would put *words* in my mouth that would be of great meaning to my fellow men, that through my *words* I would strengthen the poor, the weak and the lazy. He said I would find great success in life, inside and outside the church, through my *words*, and that I would be richly blessed with the things of this world, through my *words*.

Even before he finished I knew this was the wrong blessing to be giving to an aspiring engineer. According to this little white-haired man, whom I had never met before, my future was more about words than numbers. If I believed what he said, my life would undergo a serious change of direction at the end of my mission. But I decided rather quickly that those same promises had meaning for the here and now. I needed to do less door knocking and more preaching. I needed to give the Lord a chance to put *words* in my mouth as the patriarch promised would happen.

As we returned to Stuttgart, a plan began to formulate in my head. If *Pfarr* Herrman could schedule a hall in Reutlingen and fill it with three hundred people wanting to know more about the Mormons, I ought to be able to attract twice as many to an assembly in Stuttgart. But in Stuttgart it would be different. Missionaries would greet the people at the door and write down names and addresses for follow-up. And it would be Mormon elders, not Catholic priests, preaching from the pulpit.

The next day I found a hall near the center of the city that I could rent for two hundred *Marks* a night, about fifty dollars. Then we went to the offices of the *Stuttgarter Zeitung* newspaper where we learned we could take out a full-page advertisement, also at a cost of about fifty dollars. That night I sent a wire to Brother Crandall, a wealthy banker in my home ward in California, asking for a hundred dollars to rent a hall for a group meeting, and place a large ad in the newspaper. The money arrived by the end of the week.

The following Monday in our district meeting, I presented the plan to the rest of the missionaries. Some seemed less than enthusiastic, especially when I started assigning subjects for speeches: how Martin Luther helped prepare the world for Joseph Smith; how the church set up by Peter and the apostles went into apostasy; why we need prophets today; why the prophets in ancient America recorded their revelations on solid gold plates. Then I asked the elders for suggestions on the kinds of things we could put in the newspaper ad to attract people to our meeting.

Elder Taylor suggested a photo of the prettiest sister missionaries in the mission. Everyone liked the idea, but since we didn't have any sister missionaries in Stuttgart the suggestion was vetoed. Someone suggested we take a photo of us elders in swim suits, flexing our muscles. We agreed that would get attention, but would also get us in trouble with mission leaders. We finally decided on using a drawing of Angel Moroni blowing his horn, with the headline: *What every German wants to know about the Mormons but is afraid to ask.* The advertisement would list the titles of the various talks, with brief descriptions. The location, time and date would be at the bottom of the ad with a brief notation that refreshments would be served. By the time we finished sketching out the ad, everyone seemed pleased with our adventurous undertaking. We had a little over a week to get everything ready. I was to place the advertisement and rent the hall the next day.

For refreshments we decided to serve *Berliners*, a German-style jelly donut, a favorite of almost all missionaries. One of the elders volunteered to contract with a bakery for five hundred Berliners. Those who were assigned talks were to begin preparations immediately. The rest were assigned ushering, handshaking and crowd control activities.

Two days later I received a telegram from President Gardner telling me to call him about the upcoming public meeting we were planning. At the time I didn't know who had tipped him off, but I guessed it was one of our junior companions, an Elder Cook, the same elder who turned me in one night for taking the entire district to a John Wayne movie. I had decided it was snowing too hard to go tracting, so I had suggested we all go to the movie if the missionaries would promise to make up for the lost proselyting time on their next two diversion days. All readily agreed, including Elder Cook, but he called the mission office the next morning to confess what we had done.

I had to call President Gardner to explain everything. When I finished, there was a long pause. I thought maybe the phone had gone dead, or that he had hung up on me. Then I heard a voice asking me what I thought of the movie. I described the scene where an Indian chief in full headdress, bare-chested and carrying a bow and arrow, pulled his pinto pony to a sliding halt directly in front of John Wayne. The mighty chief raised his right arm to the square, but instead of saying the expected "How!" he gave the standard German greeting, *"Gruss Gott!"*

I told the president that westerns were my favorites back home, and I had very much wanted to see a German western, but after that greeting I didn't care if I ever saw another. He seemed satisfied with my answer. He knew from our weekly reports we were working hard, and except for Elder Cook, the missionaries were rallying behind their district leader.

When I called President Gardner to explain our public meeting, he asked what arrangements, if any, had already been made. I told him the hall and the newspaper ad had already been paid for, over a hundred dollars spent, and that it was non-refundable. He asked a few questions, then wished us good luck. He said he would come if his schedule permitted.

We printed up an invitation that looked about like the upcoming newspaper advertisement, which we gave out on the street, in restaurants, while tracting and to all our investigators. I had visions of a standing-room-only audience, especially when our advertisement appeared near the end of the front section of the newspaper just two days before the great event. We had district meetings the day before the event, and the day of the event, in which we went over all the details and rehearsed our speeches. We were so excited. We didn't invite any of the members because we didn't think there would be room for them.

The meeting was to begin at seven in the evening. We were there at six, making sure the microphone and speakers were working. We set up the refreshment table stacked high with *Berliners*, and arranged a display of *Books of Mormons* and missionary literature. I wondered what *Pfarr* Hermann would think if he could see us now.

At six-thirty we stationed elders at the doors, armed with the forms we had prepared to record our guests' addresses for follow-up. Everything was ready. Germans are notoriously punctual, so we expected the crowd to start pouring in about fifteen minutes before the hour.

At twenty before the hour I was so excited I could hardly stand it. At fifteen before the hour, I was standing in front of the building, looking up and down the street, wanting to see our first guests arrive. At ten before the hour I was beginning to wonder where our guests had gone. The street was empty, except for some children on bicycles. At five before the hour I began to feel sick. When the bell in the church down the street rang seven times, and still no guests had arrived, I felt very foolish. At five after the hour I began looking for a knife to slit my wrists. Some of the elders had gathered around the *Berliner* table, having already figured out that each elder had a quota of fifty. I remained out front, not feeling very sociable, not wanting to talk to anybody.

At quarter past the hour, I saw a lone man walking toward me with strong, confident strides. He was dressed in black. There was something familiar about his appearance. Then I noticed the high collar. He was a priest. He was *Pfarr* Hermann. I remembered he had come from Stuttgart to speak at the gathering in Reutlingen. This was his home. We shook hands. He apologized for being late due to some pressing business. He had seen our advertisement in the newspaper and had come to hear our program, and hoped he hadn't missed very much. I invited him to follow me inside.

One glance around, and *Pfarr* Hermann knew what we knew—that our entire audience consisted of one Catholic priest. Without a word he followed me to the *Berliner* table where by now all the elders had gathered. He was more than happy to help us with the formidable task of consuming five hundred jelly donuts.

"I am sorry you cannot get a refund for the newspaper advertisement," he said.

"No refund on the hall either," I mumbled, my mouth full of pastry.

We sat down in the front row, looking up at the empty podium as we continued to consume *Berliners*. In time the rest of the elders joined us. Hundreds of *Berliners* remained on the table. It would be a long night if we consumed them all.

"If you still wish to give your program, I would be delighted to hear it," *Pfarr* Hermann said.

"When I showed up at your program in Reutlingen, you were kind enough to ask me to speak," I said. "Maybe we should ask you to speak at our program."

"No. No. I am not prepared. I have not been studying the anti-Mormon brochures today."

"If the elders speak there will be only one person in the audience," I argued. "If you speak there will be ten people in the audience. Ten is better than one."

"Okay," he said rising to his feet, jumping up on the stage, and walking behind the podium.

He opened his collar, and placed a piece of paper over his left coat pocket to simulate the missionary name badge.

"Brothers and sisters," he said, in English, his accent sounding like a mixture of German and Texan. "Today I would like to tell you the story of Martin Luther, how when he was only fourteen he went in the woods to pray. An angel named Macaroni gave him a golden plate, telling him he would never have to eat on pewter ever again."

By the time he said macaroni, all the elders were

laughing like we had the greatest comedian in the world at the pulpit. But the comedy ended as quickly as it had begun.

"But this is probably not a good time for laughter," the priest continued. "You missionaries went to a lot of trouble and spent a lot of money to put on a program about your beliefs, and nobody came." He paused, looking closely at each one of us.

"But your enemy came," he continued. "Me, the priest of the people you are trying to convert. We laugh at each other's jokes, and eat *Berliners* together, but still I am your enemy."

Elder Cook and several of the missionaries were looking at me like I should do something to shut this man up. Like I should get up there and argue or debate with him. About what? I remained in my seat.

"Elder Nelson tells me there are about two hundred of you in this mission, and that every morning you pray to find converts for your church. Well, let me tell you there are more than two thousand Catholic priests in the same area who pray every morning and evening that you will not find those converts. Guess whose prayers were answered this evening?"

"We don't have to sit here and listen to this kind of garbage," Elder Cook said, standing up. Someone told him to be quiet and go get another *Berliner*. I remained in my seat.

"I will tell you why nobody came to your meeting tonight," the priest said. I nodded for him to continue because I really wanted to hear his opinion on that subject.

"You rented one of the nicest halls in Stuttgart. The news-paper gave you excellent placement for your advertisement. I guess at least fifty thousand people saw it." His voice grew louder. "The people of Stuttgart did not come to your meeting because they do not want to change churches. They do not want to hear about Joe Smith and his gold bible. I would not force my religion on people who did not want it, and neither should you. Go where people want you, or go home. The people of Stuttgart do not want you here, and after tonight I think you must agree with me." Some of the elders got up to leave. Any other time on my mission I probably would have wanted to argue with him, but not tonight. All the fight had left me.

"I only want to say one more thing," *Pfarr* Hermann said. The missionaries who were leaving turned and faced him, except Elder Cook who continued toward the door.

"You seem very proud of your sacrifice, your willingness to leave your families for two and a half years. You are a long way from home, and you do it without pay. You all think you have placed a huge sacrifice on God's altar." He paused to make sure we were listening. We were.

"You don't know what sacrifice really is," he said, his voice filling with emotion. "My two thousand brothers and I, who pray for you to fail, have placed our entire lives on the altar of God. Not just two and a half years, but all of our years." He was struggling to continue, as though the words didn't want to come out.

"While some of you dream of going home at the end of your missions, marrying your sweethearts and having children, my brothers and I have vowed celibacy until death. You may be proud of your sacrifices but you have no idea. . .." He could continue no longer. He stepped away from the podium, hopped down from the stage, and headed for the door, looking straight ahead. He did not shake our hands, nor did he say good-bye. We watched him disappear through the door. I didn't understand why he had become so emotional. Shrugging my shoulders I headed back to the *Berliner* table. I didn't think it was possible to get drunk on pastry but I was determined to give it a try on the worst night of my young life.

TEN

The next morning we were back on the doors tracting, but it wasn't business as usual. At one of the very first houses a middle-aged man came to the door quite angry with us over recent current events in America. Black people were marching to end segregation in the south. Martin Luther King and his protests were becoming commonplace. The Germans were seeing these events on their televisions too.

"How dare you come to Germany to preach Christianity. You ought to stay in America and clean up your racism first!" he shouted.

I looked at my companion, shrugging my shoulders.

"Racism? We don't have anything against the Jews, do we?"

We stepped back as the man slammed the door as hard as he could. I thought for an instant it was going to explode off its hinges and knock us down.

That afternoon a handsome young man in a tank top invited us into his small attic apartment which he shared with a wife and four very young children. The poor little wife with messy bright red hair—not yet brushed or tied up for the day—was trying to tend three steaming pots on the stove while the children demanded her attention. A little one needed changing. Another had burnt her hand and was crying. Two more were begging for bites of food. The mother not only looked tired, but frightened as well.

The man offered us seats on folding chairs where the kitchen opened into a small living room. He sat across from us, smoking a cigarette, while my companion attempted to give him the screening discussion. Occasionally, the man would break in on my companion's monologue, barking orders at the woman to get this or do that. She obeyed to the best of her ability, never seeming to question his thoughtless demands.

Finally, she was the one who interrupted our presentation, telling the man his meal was ready. He got up and walked over to the table, not indicating to us if we should join him, stay where we were, or go straight to hell. He sat down in front of his steaming plate of food—some kind of sausage with *Sauer Kraut* and potatoes—leaned forward on both elbows, and began shoveling it into his handsome mouth, totally ignoring the hungry child at each elbow. The woman was on her knees in the corner of the kitchen, trying to change one child's diaper while applying medicine to the burn on the other.

"We do not want a man like this in our church, even if he begs for baptism," I said to my companion, in German, plenty loud for everyone in the room to hear. The man looked up from his food, uncertain, as though he had heard my comment, but wasn't sure what it meant. I got up, said good-bye to the woman, and headed for the door, my companion close behind. In the doorway, I hesitated just enough to wipe my feet on the doormat before disappearing down the stairs. I was the district leader. My companion didn't question my rude behavior.

When we reached the street, Elder Burke suggested that maybe it was a bad time to be tracting, that perhaps we ought to do some laundry, or some business at the church. I promised to be more careful with my tongue, and we went back to work.

That night, after dark, we were determined to get in one more home before the end of a very hard day. We were in a single-dwelling neighborhood where most of the houses had fenced-in yards. Some of the homes had speakers installed at the front gates. You had to talk to the people through the speaker. If they agreed to let you in, they would press a button which would unlock the gate.

At one older two-story home, a man's voice came on the speaker asking us what we wanted. We told him who we were and that we would like to come in for a few minutes to share a message with him. He said that would be fine with him. His voice became very friendly. We heard a buzzing sound releasing the lock on the gate. Elder Burke pushed the gate open and stepped into the yard, then looked back at me, wondering why I was hesitating.

I was staring at the house, not seeing anything out of the ordinary, but I had the tightest feeling in the bottom of my stomach. Adrenaline had entered my bloodstream, and I didn't know why. I felt sick, like I might throw up. My heart was pounding.

Once again we could hear the same friendly male voice in the speaker, urging us to come inside. That is what we wanted to do. We pounded on doors eight or ten hours that day to get people to let us in. I couldn't figure out why I was feeling this way. As I looked at the house I couldn't put my finger on any one thing that might trigger such a response.

"I don't think we should go in," I said. "I can't tell you why."

Elder Burke looked at me for a second, then retreated from the yard. We hurried to our car and drove home. To this day I cannot give a reason for not going in that house, other than the way I was feeling. With a chip still on my shoulder from the night before, perhaps I would have punched the man. Perhaps he intended to harm us. I don't know, but over the years I have learned that when I try to ignore those kinds of feelings I am usually sorry afterward.

We hadn't been home more than ten minutes when President Gardner called. First off, he wanted to know why I had invited a Catholic priest to speak at the meeting.

"How did you know that?" I asked.

"Information has a way of getting out," he said, avoiding my question.

"Elder Cook called you. Didn't he?"

"It doesn't matter who called. I am just curious to know why you invited a priest to speak."

"Because nobody showed up. Only us elders and five hundred *Berliners*. Thought it might open the elders' eyes some to hear how a priest felt about us being in Stuttgart."

"I'm sorry nobody came. You worked so hard to make this work."

"We spent two weeks preparing our speeches, and threw away nearly five hundred marks." My voice was beginning to break. My chest was filling with emotion, and I wasn't sure why. I was tough. This shouldn't be happening, not with the mission president on the phone. I could feel cold tears on my cheeks.

"It's all right, Elder," the voice on the phone said. "You did your best, the rest is up to the Lord. Is there anything I can do for you?"

"Yes, there is," I said, gradually getting control of my voice. "Transfer Elder Cook to some far corner of the Black Forest." There was a long pause.

"Is there any particular reason you want him gone?" the president asked.

"Lots of reasons," I said. "He sleeps in church and district meetings. He stares at the pretty young girls. It's quite embarrassing. He won't learn the discussions."

"Those are the very reasons I don't want to transfer him. I want him close."

My request was declined. The president said something about Cook needing a strong companion and a strong district leader at this point of his mission. The president said he liked to keep people like Cook close to mission headquarters where they could be watched closely until they were strong enough to be good missionaries.

"Have a good night's sleep, you'll feel better about things in the morning," President Gardner said before hanging up the phone.

I didn't have a good night's sleep. My frustrations over my own failures were focused on the thorn in my side, Elder Cook. The next day at lunch, Elder Bohn, who had really enjoyed the movie and the presentation by *Pfarr* Hermann, said he had figured out a way to get Elder Cook transferred out of Stuttgart.

The next morning we visited Elder Cook and his companion before going to work. When I asked why he called the mission president to report *Pfarr* Hermann speaking at our gathering, he said there are no secrets in the work of the Lord.

"I hope you remember that when something happens in your life that you would prefer not to share with the president," I said.

"I'm sure I will never do anything I can't share with our president," he said. "I'm not like some of the missionaries I know."

"Good," I said. "I hope you never forget what you have just told me."

Fifteen minutes later, after some companion switching, Elder Bohn and I were pounding on doors with energy and enthusiasm. No bad experiences. Not only did we give three screening discussions during the morning hours, but we also made an appointment for a first lesson later in the week.

It was a beautiful day, not too hot, a gentle breeze pushing huge billowing clouds across a deep blue sky. We decided to enjoy lunch outside. When it was time we stepped into a little bakery and purchased a liter of apple cider and four of the biggest butter pretzels I had ever seen. We hurried to a little park a half a block away where we found a picnic bench near a gushing fountain surrounded by a quiet pool of water where people threw coins to make wishes. Some children with their mothers were playing on a nearby patch of grass. We began nibbling on our pretzels while tossing coins into the fountain. We had just opened the liter bottle of juice when I heard a remotely familiar female voice, behind me.

"Bruder Nelson, guten Tag."

I spun around, finding myself face to face with *Schwester* Frieda, one of the nuns I had photographed with Elder Roberts in Karlsruhe, the one who had made me lose a night's sleep while my heart was pounding. She seemed very glad to see me, like I was an old friend. Two other young nuns were standing a slight distance behind her.

"*Guten Tag,*" Elder Bohn and I said together, quickly standing up and shaking hands with the nuns. I invited them to sit across from us at the table. We pushed pretzels on napkins to the center of the table so they could share our food with us. *Schwester* Frieda told how she had been transferred from Karlsruhe to Stuttgart about a month earlier, and was assigned to a cloister a few blocks from where we lived. As she talked, I nonchalantly pressed a forefinger against the artery in my wrist to check my pulse. It seemed normal. Everything was under control.

I told the nuns how I had been transferred from Karlsruhe to Reutlingen, then to Stuttgart. They asked some questions about our work in Germany. Elder Bohn gave them a condensed version of the screening discussion. These young nuns didn't seem to be afraid of our message like older nuns usually were. And they didn't want to debate like most Catholic priests would have done under similar circumstances. When Elder Bohn was finished, he asked *Schwester* Frieda if she would do us a huge favor. She looked at the other two nuns like she wasn't sure how to respond. I had no idea what he wanted to ask her.

"I need you to write down a letter for me," he said, reaching for his notebook.

"I don't understand."

"There is a wayward missionary who needs to be taught a lesson," he explained. "He must think the letter I am going to send him is from a *Deutsche Freuline*, but missionaries don't learn to write German script. I've been looking for someone to write it down for me. I will tell you what to say."

"I think I can do that," she said, those deep green eyes looking directly into mine for the first time, as if she were seeking my approval. I looked away. I was sure she was the most beautiful woman I had ever seen, but I was determined to maintain strict control of my emotions. I was a missionary. I didn't know what Elder Bohn was trying to accomplish, but I did know I couldn't let unwanted feeling get the best of me again. There would be plenty of time for that after my mission.

She picked up the ball point pen Elder Bohn had placed on the table, positioned the piece of paper directly in front of her, and nodded for him to begin the dictation. He spoke slowly, carefully picking the words, allowing *Schwester* Frieda plenty of time to write them down.

Dear Elder Cook:

I would much rather be giving you this very personal message face to face, but you know how hard it is for a girl to talk privately to a missionary without his companion listening to every word. So I write in the hope you will understand and appreciate the sincere intent of my heart.

The happiest moments of my life occur each Sunday morning, sitting in church, looking at you sitting there on the stand, so strong, so handsome.

Sometimes I wish sacrament meeting would last all day so I could just keep looking at you hour after hour after hour. Sometimes I go out to the bathroom, hoping you will notice and come out too, without your companion, so we can talk, perhaps touch in a very legal but long handshake. I feel like I will die if I don't find out very soon if you have similar feelings for me. Until Sunday.

Your one and only in Stuttgart!

"Why are you doing this?" *Schwester* Frieda asked after addressing an envelope to Elder Cook.

"Elder Cook and Elder Nelson do not get along very well," he explained. "I fear that if Cook stays in Stuttgart, Elder Nelson may be tempted to kill him. This letter will get Cook transferred. By taking this dictation you might be saving his life. You should feel good, saving a life. Nuns do those things, you know."

"I just hope my companions don't confess what I have done," Frieda said, looking at the other nuns. They assured her they would not do any such thing.

I told them that if they got in any kind of trouble over this they could come to our church next Sunday. I assured them it would be the most interesting church meeting they would ever attend, especially watching Elder Cook's face as he searched the congregation for the author of his special letter. After shaking hands, the nuns returned to their monastery and after mailing the letter, we returned to our tracting.

I kept thinking I should not let Elder Bohn play such a dirty trick on a fellow missionary, but after what Cook had done, I just couldn't bring myself to stop such a wonderful prank.

The nuns didn't show up for sacrament meeting the following Sunday, but Elder Cook was twenty minutes early, front and center, taking one of the forward seats on the stand where he would have the best view of the congregation. His suit had been cleaned, his shirt ironed, and his hair neatly combed. He reminded me of a corpse, all dressed up for the coffin. This was the first time since I had known Elder Cook that he did not sleep in church. Neither did he slouch, fearing he might miss a glance or movement from one of the many young sisters in the congregation.

He excused himself three times during the meeting, quietly exiting through a side door for an apparent trip to the bathroom or drinking fountain. Each time he returned with a very disappointed look on his face. Elder Bohn and I thought we were going to die from our efforts not to laugh out loud, but we were determined to maintain the respectability of our positions, and held it all inside until after the meeting when we sent our companions to a dinner appointment, allowing us to escape to the safety of my car. We hooted and hollered all the way home.

That evening I received a very urgent telephone call from Elder Cook's companion, informing me that Cook was being pursued by a young sister in the Stuttgart ward. Cook couldn't contain secrecy another minute, and had shown the letter to his companion. I asked him to read to me the contents of the letter. He did a good job. The words were exactly as I remembered Elder Bohn dictating them to *Schwester* Frieda. I told the companion to call President

Gardner direct. The fewer people who got involved in such a delicate matter, the better.

The next day Elder Cook was on a train to Friedrickshaffen, about as far away from Stuttgart as one could get and still be in the South German Mission. A week later I ran into the nuns again, reported what had happened, and thanked them for their help.

ELEVEN

It seemed there was more than the usual number of priests and nuns in Stuttgart. And the vast majority weren't nearly as friendly as *Pfarr* Hermann and *Schwester* Frieda. Nearly every day a pair of elders would report some kind of discussion or argument taking place with persons of the clergy. The general rule was to avoid such debates because nobody ever seemed to win, and seldom if ever did a baptism result. But sometimes when a pair of elders would go to an appointment to give a third or fourth lesson—by now— meaning the family in question was progressing toward baptism, there would be a priest or minister in the home, ready to show the family that Mormonism couldn't stand up to conventional religion. A debate would follow, and if the elders weren't prepared, the priest or minister might end up the winner in the eyes of the family.

I decided to do some things to help prepare the Stuttgart missionaries for such debates. I announced that during our weekly district meetings we would start having debates with Catholic priests and protestant ministers. The new series of meetings would begin Wednesday at noon, and lunch would be served. I was glad Elder Cook was gone in the event the mock debates became a lot of fun. I didn't want someone calling the mission office and complaining in an attempt to stop our fun.

As the day of the first meeting approached, the big question on everyone's mind was which priest and minister would be coming to debate with us. Since I had a reputation for knowing priests and nuns, everyone assumed the real thing would be coming. They were wrong.

We didn't need real priests because we had Elder Bohn, probably one of the smartest elders in the mission, though he was not very motivated when it came to tracting. He reported more study hours than anyone in the district, but fewer tracting hours. He had been out a year longer than I had been and had perfect command of the language. And he knew the scriptures inside and out, though he hadn't memorized as many as I had. He became very excited when I secretly told him I wanted him to play the *devil's advocate* at our weekly meetings. I wanted him to be the minister the elders were going to debate.

"I'll bury them," he said, a wicked gleam in his eye.

Still I wasn't ready to begin. I wanted Elder Bohn to look like a priest or minister. One afternoon, after swapping companions, Elder Bohn and I drove to the cloister where *Schwester* Frieda lived. The elderly nun at the front gate would not let us in, but agreed to send a message to *Schwester* Frieda, who came out to greet us. I told her we were looking for priest's clothing to use in mock debates, and thought she might know where we might obtain such an outfit.

She told us we had come to the right place. Sometimes she worked in the laundry where priests from a nearby monastery brought their clothing. There was a closet in the back where they kept unclaimed items. She asked us to wait a few minutes so she could go to the laundry and check the closet.

About ten minutes later she returned, and handed us a bundle, wrapped tightly with brown butcher paper and string. The nun at the gate seemed very curious to know what *Schwester* Frieda was giving us, but Frieda wasn't about to divulge her secret, and neither were we. Someone else came to the front gate, forcing the curious nun to focus her attention elsewhere.

I asked Frieda why she had become a nun. She said, in the rural community where she grew up, most of the teachers in the little school were nuns. After an unhappy experience with a boyfriend during her mid-teens, she had decided to become a nun too, and a teacher. I asked if her commitment was for life. She said it probably was, but that it was still not too late for her to change her mind. That was all I needed to hear. I asked her for an address so I could correspond with her, to let her know how the clothes worked out, and he could contact her in the event we needed additional items for our mock debates. She pulled a pencil out of a pocket in her white apron and wrote her address on the brown paper bundle I was holding under my arm. After thanking her and shaking hands, we piled in our car and departed.

"Let the debates begin," I said as we drove away.

Before giving the bundle to Elder Bohn, I tore away the name and address on the brown wrapping paper which I deposited in a pocket close to my heart.

I wanted the new series of district meetings to be extra special, so I asked each elder to give me money in the amount of four *Marks* each, the amount a missionary would normally spend for lunch, so we could have a lunch as part of our meeting.

On the day of our first meeting the elders started arriving a little before noon. We had set up a long table where everyone could eat and work facing each other. There were three large, steaming bowls on the table. The first was full of white, red and brown *Wurst* or big hot dogs as only Germans can make them. The second bowl was overflowing with mild German *Kraut* sprinkled with round, black peppercorns. The third bowl was the largest, full of thinly-sliced boiled potatoes marinated in oil, vinegar, sugar, garlic and other spices. Tall dark-green wine bottles full of non-alcoholic grape and apple juice were in a straight line at one-foot intervals down the center of the table.

By ten after twelve all ten elders were in their seats ready to begin the feast. They could hardly believe their combined donation of only forty *Marks* had purchased so much food. After a blessing the enthusiastic elders began piling the food on their plates. As I stood back and watched, I couldn't help but feel good about what we were doing. Every face around the table looked happy. Nobody looked discouraged or homesick. The thought occurred to me that if I could figure out a way to make missionaries look this happy when tracting, the number of investigators would increase dramatically.

About the time most of the elders were stuffed too full to swallow another bite, Elder Bohn winked at me and quietly slipped from the room. Five minutes later the most intimidating Catholic priest most of us had ever seen stepped through the door. He cleared his throat to make sure he had everyone's attention. He was wearing the typical black shirt with the high collar, and a huge black robe like the ones priests often wore at mass. He wore thick silver-rimmed glasses and had a Joseph Stalin mustache under his nose. Under his arm he carried the biggest *Bible* I had ever seen. For a minute I think I was the only one in the room who knew it was Elder Bohn. His German was so perfect that even when he spoke most of the elders didn't seem to recognize him. He swaggered to one end of our banquet table and slammed down the big *Bible*. Slowly and deliberately, he looked at each one of us. He was perfect. He could have fooled anybody. He was an actor, as skilled as any I had ever seen.

Finally, Bohn looked down at his *Bible*, slowly opening it to one of the early books of Moses, studiously looking down at the holy words of God, turning the pages slowly, one at a time, finally stopping and placing his index finger on a verse. Then he looked up at us.

"What is the name of this book?" he asked, in German.

"The *Bible*," one of the elders said.

"I read somewhere that you Mormons have your own Joe Smith Bible and don't believe in this one anymore. Is that correct?"

Some of the elders were shaking their heads to indicate a negative response.

"By a show of hands, who in this room believes in the *Bible*?" All nine hands went up. Then in a louder voice:

"By a show of hands, who believes the *Bible* to be the word of God?" All nine hands went up again.

"How many of you believe that Joe Smith talked face to face with God, as one man talketh to another?" Again, every hand went up.

"Impossible," he shouted, looking down at the *Bible*,

shaking his head from side to side. "You wouldn't raise your hands like that if you had read this book. I am going to read to you from the thirty-third chapter of Exodus, verse twenty. God speaking to Moses in the wilderness.

Thou canst not see my face: for there shall no man see me, and live.

He read the same verse again, emphasizing the last eight words.

"If you believe the *Bible*, as all of you say you do, Joe Smith was lying when he said he saw God face to face. The *Bible* says no man can do that, and live. Joe Smith lived, so he is a liar. Would anyone care to differ with what God said in his holy book?"

There was silence for a long minute. Finally, a hand went up. "I believe it says somewhere else in the *Bible* that Moses saw God."

"No, it doesn't," the priest said. "God wouldn't contradict himself."

"I'm sure it says something like that," the elder persisted.

"Where?" the priest asked. The elder didn't know.

Finally, Elder Bohn's companion stood up and walked to the end of the table to stand next to the mock priest.

"*Herr* Priest, may I ask you a few questions about this Bible?"

"Of course."

"Have you read it?"

"Of course."

"Don't lie."

"Men of the cloak don't lie. I am more familiar with the contents of this book than all of you in this room put together. How do you think I found this verse that says no man can see God and live?"

"Someone might have told you about this verse, but it is obvious you haven't read the entire chapter, certainly not verse eleven, or you wouldn't be making such a ridiculous claim." The elder moved directly behind the open *Bible*, and started to read:

> *And the Lord spake unto Moses face to face, as a man speaketh unto his friend.*

Priest Bohn now had an agonized look on his face, the look of a trapped villain. The elder continued.

"This is an interesting contradiction, two verses in the same chapter of *Exodus* that appear to say opposite things. One says Moses talked with God face to face. The other says no man can see God and live. Moses talked with God, and lived. Was Moses drunk or out of his mind when he wrote *Exodus*, or is there a reasonable explanation? Can you explain this seeming contradiction?" he asked, looking at the priest. Bohn shook his head.

"Some people say we don't need prophets in modern times," the elder continued. "One of the reasons we need living prophets is to give us answers to problems like this one. Let me read what the Lord revealed to Joseph Smith in 1831 in answer to this very question:

> *"For no man has seen God at any time in the flesh, except quickened by the Spirit of God. Neither can any natural man abide the presence of God. . ."*
> *Doctrine & Covenants 67:11&12.*

"This verse makes it very clear," the elder continued, "that a natural, carnal man in his fallen state cannot endure the presence of God and live, as Moses said in verse twenty. But if that same man is *quickened by the Spirit of God* then he can endure God's presence and look at him face to face as Moses described in verse eleven. You see, Moses wasn't drunk or confused. If he made a mistake, it was not explaining this apparent contradiction. And maybe he did explain it, but the Catholic priests left that part out in the translation because they didn't understand it any more than our guest."

The elders clapped and cheered. Some of them were making marks in their *Bibles* so they would not forget what they had learned. Elder Bohn slipped out of the room, returning a few minutes later without the glasses, mustache and frock. In closing the meeting I told the elders we would do it again the following week, and as they headed out the door my companion collected another four *Marks* in lunch money from each one of them.

The next Wednesday, the feast was even better. Our main dish was a huge platter of *Wienerschnitzel*, thick pork steaks stuffed with thinly-sliced ham and Swiss cheese, rolled in whipped raw egg and spicy flour, then deep fried like they cook chicken fried steaks in America. To go with the meat we had a huge steaming bowl of *Spätzelle*, a thick, square home-made noodle, flavored with melted butter, salt, pepper, and diced green onions. A third bowl contained a rich brown gravy which could be poured over the *Wienerschnitzel* and *Spätzelle*. Again, we had tall, green wine bottles filled with apple and grape juice.

At the conclusion of our meal Elder Bohn, once again in his priestly costume, marched into the room. Like before, he slammed the big *Bible* down on the end of the table. This time he opened to one of the chapters at the end of the book, and began to read:

"For I testify unto every man that heareth the words of the prophecy of this book, If any man shall add unto these things, God shall add unto him the plagues that are written in this book. . ." Revelations 22:18

"What will happen to the person who adds to the words of this book?" Bohn asked.

No one offered to answer his question so the priest continued:

God shall add unto him the plagues that are written in this book.

"Your Joe Smith was lucky that he was shot before he was drowned in a tidal wave, crushed by an earthquake, shot by Arabs, had the flesh fall off his bones, his eyes fall out, and his skin consumed by hungry insects. These are just some of the curses mentioned by John. God made it very clear in this verse that he didn't want people adding to the *Bible*, so you Mormons come along and add a *Book of Mormon*, a *Doctrine & Covenants*, and a *Pearl of Great Price*. Not only should you be ashamed of yourselves for disobeying God, but you ought to be very scared because he promised to send you the plagues of the *Bible*."

Smug and confident, Elder Bohn looked from face to face, waiting for a response. Again, like the week before, his companion stood up and joined him at the end of the table.

"When John the Revelator wrote that," he began, "he did not have this *Bible* you see here." He picked up the big *Bible* so everyone could look at it.

"John didn't have a *Bible* at that time because there was no such book. He had only his own writing, his own revelations, his own book, which today we call *Revelation*. It's part of the *New Testament*, in fact the last book in the *New Testament*." The elder let the *Bible* fall open, allowing him to hold between his fingers a thin group of pages about an eighth of an inch thick.

"This little group of pages is John's book, the only book he had before him when he wrote that those who added to it would be cursed. I am not aware of anyone adding to John's revelations, especially not the Mormons. About three hundred years after John, the Catholics compiled all these books, at last count sixty-seven, together in one big book called the *Bible*, so maybe those Catholic scholars should get the curse for adding to John's book. But I don't think John would be opposed to people reading the books of Moses, Jeremiah, Isaiah, and so on. He just didn't want people changing his revelation."

The elders cheered. Priest Bohn looked confused. His companion continued.

"It's just too bad that when those Catholic scholars were compiling the *Bible* they didn't have trans atlantic flights and steamers. Then they would have known about the prophets on the American continent, the ones Jesus talked about when he said he had *other sheep who will hear my voice.* The prophets in America were writing down their revelations and experiences, too. If the Catholic scholars had known about them, there probably would have been books in the *Bible* with names like *Nephi* and *Alma.* Those scholars left out a lot of other books too, ones mentioned in the *Bible*, like *Zenos*, but they did the best they could. You see, John didn't want plagues sent down on those Catholic scholars, nor did he want the Mormons cursed as this gentleman has claimed. He just didn't want anyone tampering with the revelations in his book."

The elders applauded loudly as Priest Bohn slunk out of the room. They applauded the drama, and the things we were learning. Elder Bohn began to select different elders to offer the rebuttals for the attacks from the priest. He and I helped them prepare.

President Gardner called one night, telling us that a number of missionaries in their weekly reports were asking to be transferred to Stuttgart. He asked if I thought the weekly meetings were causing this response. I told him I thought the meetings were generating enthusiasm that was carrying over into the work. A lot of people were being taught. If all went well, we could end up with six baptisms for the current month. That was good, very good. I could understand why others would want to join us.

Word of our weekly dramas spread to the local members. *Bruder* Zander from the Stuttgart ward asked us to do one of our skits in his gospel doctrine class. Zander was in his late twenties, a returned missionary, and probably the best gospel doctrine teacher I have ever known. He was full of fire and enthusiasm, knowledgeable on many religious subjects. He had defected from East Germany eight years earlier, but when his fiancé tried to follow, she was captured at the border and sent home. *Bruder* Zander continued to send her money, and whenever we visited his apartment, there were maps spread out on the kitchen table as he made plans for her repeated escape attempts which always seemed to fail.

Elder Bohn was brilliant, carrying the old Bible, dressed in his frock, with the mustache and glasses. He fooled the gospel doctrine class too, at least the first week.

For the first time since coming to Germany, I felt like I was really enjoying the work. It was easier to get up in the morning and get going. It was almost fun. I felt like I was building lasting human relationships with fellow missionaries, members and investigators. And as impossible as it may seem, I even had that feeling at times that I didn't want my mission to end. My friends at college would think I was absolutely nuts.

While driving home one evening, after interviewing an older woman for baptism, I could not stop the tears from streaming down my cheeks. The spirit had been so strong. She was such a good person, so deserving of the blessings of the gospel. I don't know how I could have felt any happier, for her and for me. I had never felt this way before my mission.

A few weeks later we had an interesting conversation with a young man who was being baptized. He asked if my companion and I were the ones who had brought the baptismal papers to his house that afternoon when he was gone. I said we were the ones. He told us that when he got home the landlady said two of the strangest young men had brought him some papers. He asked what was so strange about the young men. She said "They glowed like angels."

It had been our diversion day and we had taken our weekly bath that morning, but I'm sure the glow experienced by that woman was more than physical cleanliness. It was as though the hand of the Lord was resting on our shoulders at times. We could sense it, and sometimes others could too.

I knew I had finally achieved the feeling that missionaries are supposed to have, but the thing that would bring me back to reality was remembering Elder Kimball's blessing, to bring *a thousand souls* to the truth. How could I be happy when that was not happening? Even with all the good that was going on around me, the promise of *a thousand souls* was still a million miles away. I knew the discussions and the language. I had memorized five hundred scriptures. I could do more pushups and give more screening discussions than anyone I knew. But still I came up short. I was either not doing enough, or I needed to do something different, and I didn't know what that was.

On the night American President John F. Kennedy was shot, I was working with Elder Krueger, who possibly had more faith than any missionary I knew. When I first met him, it was late fall, and he had just given his winter coat to an investigator. He had thought the investigator needed it more than he did. I asked Krueger if he had enough money to buy a new one. He did not, but he smiled and said the Lord would provide. He wasn't worried about it, and told me I should not worry. A week later a woman he had baptized in another city heard what he had done and mailed him a brand new coat.

"See," he said, "the Lord provides."

We couldn't do any teaching that night because all that the people wanted to talk about was the American president. Flags were at half staff. People in the streets were crying. It was as if the world had suddenly stopped. I remember wondering if the people in America were as shocked by this as were the German people. Kennedy had come to Berlin and said *"Ich bin ein Berliner,"* and the Germans loved him, possibly more than their own leader at the time.

We knocked off early that night, and as Elder Krueger and I were visiting, I told him about Elder Kimball's blessing, and how frustrated I was that I couldn't find *a thousand souls.* He just smiled, and said, "Have faith, Brother, the Lord will provide a way."

"But time is running out," I complained.

"You are doing your best."

"My best isn't good enough."

"Yes, it is. The rest is up to the Lord."

Not very long after that, as I was contemplating our weekly scripture bashes with Priest Bohn, and how much the elders enjoyed these debates, the thought occurred to me that perhaps we could take our fun to the German people, our prospective converts. Everyone likes a good fight. The enthusiasm for our debates was similar to that of sports fans before a championship game. Germans loved their soccer matches, so they ought to love a great debate over religion, something they hadn't experienced in a long time. Even the Catholics were proud of Martin Luther for standing up to the pope. It was time to start a new fight over religion, one that would capture the interest of every non-Mormon in

Stuttgart, and fill our appointment books with the names of people wanting to be taught the gospel.

I told Elder Bohn to write me the meanest, most entertaining, Mormon-bashing letter he could come up with—that he'd better make it good, because I intended to get it published in the *Stuttgarter Zeitung* newspaper. I said this was just between me and him. I didn't want anyone else to know about it, especially not President Gardner. I didn't have to ask twice. With a gleam in his eye, Elder Bohn promised to hand me a literary masterpiece in two days.

TWELVE

Elder Bohn didn't let me down. The translation of his letter reads as follows:

Dear Editor:

Having recently returned to the Stuttgart area after an extended period of religious study in The United States, I am shocked and saddened at the expanded efforts of the Mormons to round up German war widows to become their plural wives in Utah. The Mormons believe Germany's millions of war widows comprise a "field that is white, already to harvest." The reference to color is an indication that Mormons don't like people of non-white races. Following the war, the Mormons sent millions of pounds of food to Germany to insure the cooperation of our government in allowing them to brainwash our women. Once in America, the female convert meets disappointment and heartache. Instead of marrying the handsome young missionary who converted her, she usually ends up in the crowded harem of a fat old man suffering from gout and colic.

A convert from Heilbronn went to America to marry her young missionary, which marriage took place in the temple in Salt Lake City. Her regrets came immediately after the wedding when she was told she had to spend the wedding night with her missionary's bishop. She refused and tried to flee, eventually jumping from one of the temple windows and drowning in the Great Salt Lake.

The Mormons have a very good reason for sending their younger men to do the recruiting. When they made their pact with the Devil in founding their church, old Lucifer required the Mormon men to grow cow-like horns to prepare them for ministering in the kingdoms of hell. This horn growth usually isn't noticeable until the middle years, and never in young men under twenty five. So they send their young men to find women to populate the harems of Utah. These missionaries may appear as harmless as lambs, but in reality they are wolves in sheep's clothing.

Pfarr Johann Gläzer

The letter was written in longhand, like an American would write it. German longhand is very different in appearance. I didn't want an editor seeing the American style and guessing a missionary had composed it. I had two choices, type it on a German typewriter, or get one of the natives to copy it by hand. I decided on the latter, thinking that when the editor saw the composition in native script he would assume a German had written it.

I sent a note to *Schwester* Frieda at the cloister, asking her to meet us at the park on a certain day at a certain time.

I told her the truth, that we needed her to copy a letter in the German script so we could properly submit it to a newspaper. She and another young nun showed up at the park at the prescribed time. While my companion was giving a screening discussion to her companion, *Schwester* Frieda copied the note. Of course she wanted to know if any of the accusations in the letter were true. I assured her they were not.

"Not even the part about the horns?" she asked.

People reading this forty years later might think the horn business more than a little silly, something normal people wouldn't begin to believe, but in Germany in 1963, many of the missionaries I knew had been asked more than once about their horns. And the story about the woman jumping out the temple window, I had heard more than once too. Apparently stuff like this was still being published in a book or brochure being distributed by the clergy to the people to protect them from what their leaders perceived as the Mormon threat.

I invited *Schwester* Frieda to touch a spot on my head, above the right eye and behind the hairline, to see if she could feel a bump or nub where horn growth might begin. She was reluctant at first, but finally reached out, extending a single forefinger, gently exploring the area on my head where a horn might begin to grow.

"Do you feel anything?" I asked.

"No," she said.

"Try a little more to the right."

"Okay"

"Now do you feel anything?"

"No."

"I'm sure you feel something."

"No," she said as she explored a few other spots.

"Don't you even feel a little foolish?"

She withdrew her hand, a wry smile on her face.

"It really is silly," she finally said. "Not only that people like me are tempted to believe, but that those who tell us these things think we are gullible enough to believe."

I asked her how her studies were progressing. She said she was working hard. She also said she knew *Pfarr* Hermann, the priest who had attended our failed meeting. Though he liked us as people, he was confident our work would fail.

"What do you think?" I asked.

"I am only nineteen. I do not have opinions about such things. You obviously think you will succeed. I suppose I will wait and see, though at the present, I think *Pfarr* Hermann is probably right."

"Did you read the *Book of Mormon* I gave you?" I asked.

"No. I knew I would get in trouble for having it, so I threw it away. Perhaps later I will read your book, but not now."

It was time for the nuns to return to the cloister, but I still had an important item to discuss with *Schwester* Frieda.

"Will you promise to keep this a secret, that you copied this letter in German script for me?"

"Why is this important?"

"It just is."

"I didn't tell anyone about the other letter, the one the missionary thought was from the girl at church."

"Thank you, but will you promise not to tell anyone about this letter today?"

"I'm not sure why this is so important to you," she said. "But I give you my promise."

While the nuns were returning to the cloister, my companion and I mailed the letter to the newspaper.

For about a week, we checked the newspaper every day to see if the letter was published. Nothing. I guessed the editor decided against starting a religious debate, or he suspected that the letter was a publicity stunt on the part of the Mormons, but for the life of me I couldn't figure out why he would think that. I felt like I would give about anything to know his thinking on this. We had gone to a lot of trouble, and nothing happened.

One morning as we were tracting a high-rise apartment building, about two weeks after mailing the letter, a woman who opened one of the doors began acting in a very strange manner as we attempted to ask her the survey questions. She kept rising on her toes, at the same time stretching her neck as if she were trying to get a better look at the tops of our heads.

I ran my hand through my hair, wondering if perhaps I had lice, or that maybe a bird might have deposited something on my head that morning. I didn't notice anything unusual, so I asked the woman if there was a problem. I told her I was very curious to know what she was looking at. I smiled. She smiled back.

"I've never seen horns on a human before, not even little tiny ones," she said, being as polite as she could possibly be, obviously worried that she might offend us.

My companion and I grinned at each other. I wanted to shout. The newspaper had finally published the letter.

"I'll make a deal with you," I said to the woman, lowering my voice to a whisper so none of the neighbors could hear. "If you'll let us in so I can sit in a chair, I'll let you examine the top of my head."

She looked up and down the hall to make sure no one was watching, then ushered us in. She showed us the letter to the editor in the newspaper. After running her fingers through my hair she stepped back and laughed.

"I just knew it couldn't be true," she said. "But. . ." She laughed again. We told her the part about our wanting to recruit plural wives wasn't true either, then gave her the screening discussion. She gave us cookies and milk. We had a great visit. She was so nice, but didn't want future appointments to hear our discussions. Changing churches was not an option for her to consider, but we were welcome to come back any time we felt hungry for some good cookies.

The offer to let people touch our budding horns got us in three more homes that morning. I called an emergency meeting with the other missionaries to go over this new door approach. Everyone already knew about the letter in the newspaper because they were getting asked about horns and plural wives too. One of the elders picked up some cheap rings at a store, and was wearing four of them side by side on the ring finger on his left hand. When someone would ask him about polygamy, he would show them the rings. Touching them one at a time, he would say "Jane, Mary, Ruth and Elizabeth. If you'll invite us in I'll tell you all about it."

Over time we discovered that it was usually women who asked about the horns, while the men were more curious about polygamy. In some cases, because of the letter, older women seemed more frightened to talk to us, but overall we were being invited into a lot more homes, giving more screening discussions and making more appointments for discussions. It seemed everyone had read the outrageous letter. It had done a good job for us, but it was only part of the plan. It was time to return fire. I composed a rebuttal letter, from me, in good old American schoolboy longhand.

Dear Editor:

In his recent letter to the editor, Herr Gläzer forgot to mention that the Heilbron woman who jumped from the window of the Mormon temple and drowned in the Great Salt Lake was a world-class long jumper. How else could she have covered a distance of a dozen kilometers in a single leap?

Gläzer's claim that Mormons are rounding up war widows for Salt Lake harems is outrageous. Any normal person knows the Mormons stopped rounding up plural wives in the 1890s. I grew up in Utah and during my entire life I never met a Mormon with more than one wife.

Gläzer needs to start telling the truth, if he hasn't suffered too much brain damage from drinking his own bath water.

His claim that Mormons grow horns is a claim too ridiculous to be argued in the pages of a newspaper. The ten young Mormons presently working in Stuttgart invite residents with scientific curiosity to feel the tops of their heads to see if there really are nubs or bumps where little horns are beginning to grow.

As for Herr Gläzer, I am confident his libelous and slanderous attack on an innocent and God-fearing people has earned him a plunge into the fiery depths of Hell, perhaps earning him a spot at the right hand of old Lucifer himself.

Elder Nelson
Stuttgart Missionary

This time, after dropping the letter in the mailbox, there was not so long a wait before it was published. I was sure glad the people in Stuttgart liked to read their newspaper. Some people asked about the horns, but most just laughed over the debate they were following in the newspaper. People didn't seem so reluctant to talk to us. They seemed surprised that we were such good sports over Gläzer's broadside. Most seemed pleased that we had responded with humor and enthusiasm, instead of defensive bitterness. We were getting in more homes and teaching more lessons.

After a few days Elder Bohn wrote a new letter from the fictitious *Herr* Gläzer. He made fun of the *Book of Mormon* which "Joe Smith said he copied from a pile of solid gold plates he found while taking a walk in the woods, but when the people who saw the book wanted to see the gold plates, they had mysteriously disappeared." Before sending it to the newspaper I had *Schwester* Frieda copy it in the German longhand style.

In my response I reported that a number of people saw

the gold plates, and that their names are published in the *Book of Mormon*. I further described how impossible it would be for a fourteen-year-old boy, without any formal schooling to write a thousand-year history of three civilizations on two continents including numerous doctrinal essays on difficult religious subjects like atonement, the fall of Adam, faith, repentance, baptism, prayer and other subjects that challenged even the most skilled theologians. Again, I said there was no need to argue the merits of the *Book of Mormon* in the pages of a newspaper because anyone who really wanted to assess the truthfulness and value of the book could evaluate it themselves by reading a free copy from the missionaries. But if *Herr* Gläzer asked for a *Book of Mormon* I would drop an entire case on his foot.

It wasn't long until it seemed everyone in Stuttgart was following the Mormon debate in the newspaper. We couldn't eat lunch, ride a street car, or go to the store without someone asking us about the debate. We were teaching and baptizing like never before. I should have been satisfied, but I wasn't. I was still haunted with Elder Kimball's promise of *a thousand souls*. I kept thinking there had to be a way to use the newspaper debate as a stepping stone to something bigger and better.

At the end of his next letter, *Herr* Gläzer accused me of being a fancy writer, but if I had the courage to meet him face to face he would point out the errors of Mormonism with such force that I would be humbled to tears and scamper back to Utah with my tail between my legs. Of course, in my next letter I welcomed the chance to once and for all expose his many lies and send him straight to hell on a greased flagpole. At the end of the letter the editor announced when and where the debate would take place—the same building I had rented before, and the public was invited to enjoy the fireworks.

This time we didn't have to waste my banker's money on a huge advertisement. From the letters, everyone knew about the debate. From the comments we were getting on the street, we knew a lot of people were coming. This time we ordered a thousand *Berliners*. We printed sign-up sheets so we would get the name and address of everyone who entered the building. We ordered ten cases of *Books of Mormon* and additional boxes of fliers from the mission office. Elder Bohn and I spent many hours planning an entertaining debate between *Herr* Gläzer and me. We were determined to make a show of it. We knew reporters and photographers from the *Stuttgarter Zeitung* would be there, and we hoped to see a huge article in the paper the day after.

I had read stories about Wilford Woodruff and other missionaries in the early days of the Church, converting entire congregations. I was beginning to believe we were going to pull off something like that in Stuttgart in 1963. Perhaps this would be the first big step on the way to finding *a thousand souls.*

THIRTEEN

The second meeting was just like the first one in that *Pfarr* Hermann was the first to arrive, this time about twenty minutes early. I greeted him out in the street. We shook hands like before, but he didn't seem nearly as friendly this time. He looked different. His eyes were bloodshot. His healthy complexion had become pink and puffy. He looked like he had lost weight. Something was wrong.

"Did you come to debate with us?" I asked, cheerfully.

"No, just to watch."

"Do you think anyone will come this time?"

"No doubt about it, but amidst all the seemingly false claims, I think *Herr* Gläzer made at least one very accurate statement."

"And what was that?"

"When this is over you will be scampering back to Utah with your tail between your legs." He was serious, no smile on his face. He was not kidding.

His statement stopped me in my tracks. I thought I had been nurturing a pleasant relationship with this Catholic cleric. Now this. Did he really think the fictitious *Herr* Gläzer would defeat me in a debate? Even so, he shouldn't have said that. Friends, even remote ones, didn't say things like that without a smile on the face.

"I guess we'll just have to wait and see," I said. He turned and entered the building.

Next came two nuns I had seen on other occasions with Sister Frieda. When I greeted them and asked why *Schwester* Frieda was not with them, they looked away and didn't answer. After entering the building they seated themselves next to *Pfarr* Hermann.

All of a sudden it seemed like the street was full of people. Some came alone, some in groups. All were greeted by missionaries and took cards to fill out as they entered the building. Soon the lobby was full of people and the seats were filling up quickly. I looked at my watch. We still had ten minutes before it was time to start.

When it was time to begin, all the seats were full, and a few people were standing against the wall. Our little debate in the newspaper had produced a larger crowd than *Pfarr* Hermann had attracted in Reutlingen. He was sitting near the back, a nasty scowl on his face. I figured he had been friendly to us as long as he thought we were harmless and ineffective. Now that it appeared we were on the verge of converting large numbers of people, we were suddenly the enemy. So be it.

A missionary stepped up to the microphone and gave an opening prayer. Then he introduced *Herr* Gläzer. Elder Bohn walked out from behind the curtains, wearing the frock *Schwester* Frieda had given us, the mustache and glasses, and carrying the big *Bible* under his arm. The audience applauded. There were a few hisses and boos. He waved at the audience.

Next, they introduced me. As I walked from behind the curtain, everyone started to laugh. I had glued two plastic cow horns to a pair of ear muffs, the kind where the two sides are attached with a metal band extending over the top of the head. With the horns in place I walked from behind the curtain. It looked like real horns were growing out of both sides of my head, just above the ears. There were gasps and awes from the audience followed by loud laughter.

When I reached the front of the stage, I removed the horns and handed them to *Herr* Gläzer.

"You can keep these to remind you of your wars with the Mormons," I said. "You may want to hang them over your fireplace like a deer trophy. Or after you join the Mormons, you may want to wear them to church so you will feel at home among the high priests." This comment brought both cheering and jeering from the audience. It seemed everyone was having a great time. With the microphone firmly in hand I stepped behind the podium.

"Before we begin, I would like to call *Herr* Gläzer's attention to a verse in the *Old Testament* that has a special message for him tonight, a word of caution that will save him from a very embarrassing situation." I asked him to read *Isaiah 6:5*:

"Woe is me for I am undone...," he read from the big *Bible.*

Only a few people laughed at first, but words of explanation spread quickly through the audience. By the time the red-faced Gläzer turned his back to the audience so he could zip himself up, everyone was enjoying a good laugh. Bohn and I had planned this ahead of time, and it had the desired effect on the audience. This was like professional wrestling, more of a show than a real competition, except the audience didn't seem to know it, at least not yet.

"We are having such a good time," I said, "that I hate to get serious. But that is exactly what we have to do. *Herr* Gläzer has made some serious claims against the church of God, and it's about time he was held accountable for his false claims."

About this time a reporter and photographer from the *Stuttgarter Zeitung* entered the rear of the hall. *Pfarr* Hermann left his seat so he could join the reporter in the aisle. Hermann was talking while the reporter was taking notes. Several other people joined them. The photographer moved to the front of the hall so he could get some good pictures of me and Gläzer.

Herr Gläzer began the debate by claiming the Mormons had no authority from God to do what they do. The Catholics could trace their priesthood back to Peter, and the Protestants could trace their authority back to Martin Luther. The Mormons couldn't trace their priesthood any further back than Joe Smith, and therefore had no authority to bless, baptize, hold meetings, or do anything else in the name of God, whose house was a house of order. The Mormons were flagrantly ignoring the need for priesthood authority and order in God's church.

I agreed with him that priesthood was important, then told the story of the restoration of the Aaronic priesthood through John the Baptist, and the Melchizedek priesthood through Peter, James and John. Some of the people in the audience seemed a little bored with this, as if they wanted to see Gläzer and me punching each other. But we plunged ahead, debating the usual subjects like polygamy, golden plates and the need for a *Book of Mormon*, infant baptism, word of wisdom, baptism for the dead, even the law of the tithe. Several times I asked other missionaries to offer rebuttals. Of course, they had been coached ahead of time and were well-prepared. Each missionary, including myself, ended each response with fervent testimony as to the truthfulness of our comments.

We all knew that true conversion did not begin or end with showmanship or debate. In the end our only success, if any, would come from the spirit bearing witness, touching the hearts of those ready to receive the gospel, so they would know from warm feelings within, that our words were true. We had worked and prayed with all our hearts to make this event a success, the rest was up to the Lord.

In the middle of all this the reporter and photographer left. At the end of the debate, *Herr* Gläzer, feigning anger and frustration, turned and disappeared behind the curtain. We didn't want him mingling with the audience following the presentation, risking the discovery of his true identity.

After a closing prayer and a blessing on the *Berliners*, the missionaries mingled with the audience, writing down more names and making appointments to teach. *Pharr* Hermann, before leaving, tapped me on the shoulder and reminded me that a reporter had been present and that I should watch for the resulting article in the newspaper.

Before we were through, we had accumulated over three hundred leads, made nearly forty teaching appointments, and given away two cases of the *Book of Mormon*. Everyone had to agree, the evening was a smashing success.

We missionaries had good reason to be especially happy.

With so many new people to contact and teach, we would have little time for tracting, at least for the next few weeks. This was like a well-deserved vacation. And unlike our first meeting at the hall, when we locked up at the end of this evening there were no leftover *Berliners* to take home.

Our hard-earned glory was short-lived. The article in the newspaper the next day accused us of trickery and deceit. It explained how we had duped the people of Stuttgart into coming to our meeting by staging a fake debate in the newspaper, and how we had deployed the same deception to present a live debate in front of a foolhardy audience of ignorant Germans.

The article included a very silly picture of me wearing the fake horns, and another unflattering photo of *Herr* Gläzer with a caption explaining that he was really Elder Bohn from Salt Lake City dressed in a holy Catholic gown stolen from a local monastery. It said missionary work was an ideal training ground for young Mormons who wanted to learn how to do magic shows, sell used cars, or do skits on late night television. *Pfarr* Hermann was quoted in several places. Of course he had nothing good to say about us or our church.

It was the worst article about the Mormons I had ever seen, and it was all my fault. So much for the dream of converting *a thousand souls*. I figured the work in Stuttgart had been set back at least a hundred years.

I couldn't help but wonder how the newspaper found out about Elder Bohn's fake identity. The only one outside our close circle of missionaries who knew about it was *Schwester* Frieda. I couldn't believe she would turn on me like this. Our relationship was all it could be, and no more, considering the strict rules controlling both of our lives. Elder Cook was gone, and none of the other missionaries would have leaked something like this to the press.

I remembered *Pfarr* Hermann's comment about me returning to Utah with my tail between my legs. I remembered his reminder to be sure and look for the newspaper article. But he didn't know about Elder Bohn. I hadn't told him a thing. Yet, it appeared he was the source of the information in the article.

Late that night I received a call from President Gardner. He had read the article. He said it was the meanest attack against the Church he had seen during his mission, that he was considering taking all the missionaries out of Stuttgart for at least six months, hoping this might blow over.

I begged him not to close the city. Good people were being taught. Baptisms were being planned.

"They may cancel when they read the article," he said. "This is a terrible thing for the Church."

"We were only doing our best to find more people to teach. We didn't know it was going to backfire."

"But you staged a fake debate, a monstrous deception."

"I don't mean disrespect, sir, but our model is your *Black Book*. We conduct fake surveys every day."

There was silence on the phone.

"I will postpone the decision to close the city," he said when the conversation resumed. "But effective immediately, you are relieved of district leader duties and are being transferred to Esslingen. You go there day after tomorrow."

"But. . ."

"Please don't argue with me," he said. "This is the right thing to do. Let us know of your arrival time so you can be picked up at the train station." He hung up the phone.

The next morning I didn't get out of bed until after seven. It was the first time since coming to Germany that I didn't get up before six. I just couldn't seem to find the strength to roll out of the sack. I said my prayers, but skipped the pushups. I didn't review the discussions or my five hundred scriptures. I dragged my trunk out from under the bed and started throwing stuff in it.

I knew I was behaving badly, but I also believed I would get over it. I had made some wonderful friends and baptized some excellent people. None of that had changed. And if I worked hard in Esslingen, maybe I would find a few more wonderful people before it was time to go home. I could live with that.

We were out the door at nine sharp. There were members, friends and missionaries I wanted to say good-bye to, people who meant a lot to me. I might never see them again. I figured some of the visits would be awkward, considering the circumstances which caused my departure, but I could live with that too.

Our first stop was Elder Bohn's apartment. He shook my hand firmly and thanked me for some of the most memorable moments of his mission.

"It was a wild ride," he said. "More fun than is legal for missionaries to have."

He handed me the black frock, once again wrapped in brown butcher paper.

Our next stop was the cloister where I hoped to return

the frock. The older nun at the gate looked at us with suspicion when I asked to see *Schwester* Frieda. Obviously, the nun knew about the article in the newspaper. She seemed surprised that we were not already dead. I told her I was leaving town, and wished to return something. She said she would return the bundle for me, but when I refused to give it to her, she reluctantly sent a message requesting *Schwester* Frieda to come to the front gate.

When *Schwester* Frieda finally arrived, I noticed that her eyes were red, as though she had been crying. We stepped out on the sidewalk, out of hearing of the other nun. I handed her the frock and told her I was being transferred to Esslingen and would probably never see her again. She did not express any regrets, but told me that *Pfarr* Hermann had been transferred to Esslingen too.

I wanted to tell her I didn't need any more bad news like that, that I never wanted to see Hermann again, not as long as I lived. But I didn't tell her any of this. I knew she could be called inside any minute. I wanted to know that she wasn't my enemy too, that she hadn't been involved in leaking information about the staged debate to the press. I asked her if she knew how the reporter found out about *Herr* Gläzer.

"I confessed everything to *Pfarr* Hermann," she said, not looking even a little bit guilty. "He told the reporter."

"But why?" I asked, feeling that I had been betrayed, wanting her to feel guilty and ashamed for what she had done. Instead she became angry.

"I am Catholic. You used me in your war against my church. You made me feel like a traitor. You should be ashamed."

"I never twisted your arm to do anything."

"I know. It all seemed so harmless at first. But then it was big. Everyone in Stuttgart was reading the letters. Hundreds came to your meeting. I had to confess my sins in helping you."

"If you don't feel bad about what you have done, then why have you been crying?" I asked.

"You think the whole world revolves around you and your silly missionary work. Well, it doesn't. My crying has nothing to do with you." Without another word, she tucked the frock under her arm, turned and ran back into the cloister.

"Guess we've seen the last of *Schwester* Frieda," I said to my companion. We got in our car and drove away. While we were having lunch, I removed the piece of paper containing her address. I was going to throw it away, but couldn't bring myself to do it. I slipped it back in my pocket. Still, I felt betrayed. I had trusted her too much. That had been wrong, and I figured God was punishing me for it. I was a big boy, and guessed I might survive this too. I didn't waste any time wondering what it might have been that caused her to cry.

The next morning I was dropped off at the train station an hour before my scheduled departure. My companion and the elders with him had a lot to do, closing down two apartments and bringing in some new elders from mission headquarters, so we said our quick good-byes and they were on their way, leaving me alone to wrestle with my troubles. I began pacing back and forth like a caged animal at the zoo.

Before long I heard someone call my name. I recognized the voice. It was *Bruder* Zander, the gospel doctrine teacher in the Stuttgart ward. I had stopped by his flat the night before, to say good-bye, but he had not been home. Now he was at the train station. I was glad he had come.

After shaking his hand, I noticed that his eyes were red just like *Schwester* Frieda's had been. Something was bothering him, and this time I was sure it had nothing to do with me, and what *Schwester* Frieda had called my little narrow world of silly missionary work. I asked him what was wrong.

He started telling me the same story he had told me before, how he had escaped East Germany eight years earlier, but how his fiancé had been stopped at the border and sent home. He had sent money to her, and twice more she had tried to cross the border, each time being caught by border guards and sent home. He had continued sending her money, but now she was too afraid to try again. He was thirty years old. His biological clock was ticking, his fiancé's too. He felt he was going to go crazy if the situation wasn't somehow resolved. He had considered crossing back over into East Germany, marrying his fiancé, and living with the communists the rest of his life. But his freedom had been won at too high of a price to just give it back, even if it meant being with the one he loved.

"So what should I do, Elder Nelson?" he asked.

"You're asking the wrong person if you want to know about matters of the heart," I said, explaining that I had only had about a dozen dates in my whole life, and never more than three with the same girl. I didn't even have a girlfriend to write to. I wasn't qualified to answer questions about love.

"I am in a stalemate," he said, emotion in his voice. "I have been fasting and praying for eight long years, and seem incapable of resolving this. I need help."

"Why do you think I can help?" I asked.

"Only a feeling, but a strong one. I believe you can tell me what to do, or through you, the Lord can tell me what to do. You are his ordained minister."

"I don't suppose you have read the newspapers lately?" I asked.

"I saw the article about Elder Bohn dressing up like a priest, if that's what you are referring to."

"I have disgraced the Church, and embarrassed the mission president. I have been relieved of my duties and banished to Esslingen. They could have sent me home. I am hardly the person anyone should come to for spiritual advice."

"You are in good company," he said, smiling for the first time.

"What is that supposed to mean? I am alone, shunned and disgraced."

"You are in good company. When Joseph Smith founded the Church, every newspaper in America was editorializing against him. When Brigham Young established Zion in the Rocky Mountains, every newspaper and every minister in America rallied against him, even the United States Army and Congress. The little article in the *Stuttgarter Zeitung* is but a drop in the bucket compared to all that other bad publicity."

"You are the ultimate optimist," I conceded, "trying to convince me that some very bad publicity is somehow very good."

"No, it was bad. But it always happens when men of God

stir things up so a lot of good can happen. Satan suddenly wakes up, rallies his forces, and fights back. I have seen all the new investigators in my class every Sunday. I have been to many of the baptisms which are rolling in on a weekly basis. Your good works have awakened the devil. He struck back. That means you are doing something right. Can't you see?"

"I feel a lot better than I did an hour ago," I said.

"I know I'm right. Now tell me what I should do. Should I return to East Germany?"

"No," I said.

"Then I should keep sending her money?"

"No. All you need to do is call *Schwester Whatshername* tonight and invite her to have dinner with you."

I now call her *Whatshername* because after forty years I cannot remember her real name. Elder Krueger taught her the discussions. It seemed she had a million questions and often didn't seem satisfied with the answers. She was young and pretty, but had a tormented look about her. I'll never forget the day she showed up to be interviewed for baptism. I didn't recognize her. After a lot of praying and fasting, the light finally came on, and her total countenance changed. She literally looked like a different person, now that she was filled with the Spirit. I feel bad calling her *Whatshername*, but it seems wrong to give her a fictional name.

"I hardly know her," *Bruder* Zander choked.

"She comes to your class each week. You came to her baptism. You know her well enough to have dinner with her."

"She knows I'm engaged."

"Yeah, to a woman you haven't seen in eight years."

"You think I should marry *Schwester Whatshername?*"

"I think you should ask her to have dinner with you."

"How long have you felt this way?"

"Since the day I interviewed her for baptism. I had never seen anyone's countenance change that much. That's when I started thinking you and she could be very happy together. So, will you ask her to have dinner with you?"

"I'll think about it."

"That's not good enough. Will you ask her today?"

"I will do it," he finally said. We shook hands, he threw his arms around me, then skipped out of the *Bahnhoff.*

FOURTEEN

Serving in Esslingen wasn't nearly as bad as I thought it was going to be. The Neckar River meandered through town, with a number of very old stone bridges allowing people to cross back and forth. Most of the houses were old too, evidence there had not been a lot of allied bombing here during World War II. The traditional construction style consisted of massive timbers placed in upright, horizontal and diagonal positions, the inside space filled with brick and plaster. Portions of the old city wall remained in place too. Many of the streets were still paved with cobblestones. Parts of the city looked like post cards from eighteenth century Germany.

Next to the river, near the middle of the town, was a huge church many hundreds of years old. There were two very high stone towers at one end, the tops connected by a suspended and enclosed walkway. But the towers didn't match in architecture and construction, as if two rival builders were bound and determined to build something unique and different, a situation comparable to the Mormon Church replacing one of the towers on the Salt Lake temple with a rounded dome like on the mosques in Palestine. I decided if I ever visited this church in Esslingen I would be sure to ask about the towers. But I didn't think I would do that because I might run into *Pfarr* Hermann, since he was in Esslingen too. I didn't want to see him again, not ever.

Our living quarters consisted of a flat with a balcony overlooking the river, the huge church, and part of the old city wall. The view from our balcony was good enough to make a post card. Since the balcony faced east, it was perfect for outside study on summer mornings. Without question, this place was more aesthetically pleasing than any of the other places I had lived since coming to Germany.

My new companion, Elder Bateman, hadn't been in Germany very long, so he was still very humble, working hard to memorize the discussions and learn the language. Like me, he didn't seem to care much what he ate, as long as there was plenty of it. And he didn't seem like the type to shy away from a little hard work. We were going to get along just fine. I began to get excited about the new assignment. No big responsibilities, just Elder Bateman and I riding our bikes through the post card scenery, finding and teaching good people. As soon as we started having baptisms, President Gardner would be sorry he ran me out of Stuttgart. But we'd have to hurry. It was about time for the president to go home.

My companion hadn't read the *Bible* before his mission, so we started reading that during our study together. We began with the *New Testament* because there are more verses there that can be used in missionary work.

The person who has never lived the missionary life might think that spending an hour with another person reading in the *Bible* every morning, is a boring activity. In reality, this time together was anything but boring, like the time we were reading *Mark 3: 29:*

But he that shall blaspheme against the Holy Ghost hath never forgiveness, but is in danger of eternal damnation. . ..

Elder Bateman got very excited, as though a light had just gone on.

"This explains why people who swear never say Holy Ghost!" he said.

"What?" I asked, looking up from my *Bible*.

"All my life I've heard people take God's and the Lord's name in vain, and ten different versions of the S, B and F words," he continued, getting more excited. "But I've never heard anyone say 'Holy Ghost!' This verse explains it. They'd face eternal damnation. That's why they don't do it."

"Do you believe that?" I asked.

"Sure. It's explained right here in the *Bible*."

I got up from my chair. I was in my stocking feet. I walked over to the table where we eat, and kicked the closest leg of the table, hard enough to hurt, but not hard enough to break my toe.

"Holy Ghost!" I said, dancing around on one foot, holding up my injured foot. Elder Bateman's eyes got really big, but he didn't say anything as I returned to our study desk. We had a pretty good discussion on what it really meant to *blaspheme against*, or deny the Holy Ghost or Spirit of God.

About a week later we were reading *Luke 11:27-36,* the story of Jesus blessing a man possessed of evil spirits who would break the chains confining him and run naked in the wilderness. The spirits asked to be left alone, but when they realized Jesus was going to cast them out anyway, they said their name was *Legion*. They asked if they could enter the bodies of a bunch of pigs grazing on a nearby hill. Jesus said they could, and when they did, the pigs stampeded into a lake and *choked* or drowned.

Elder Bateman could not continue reading. He had to know why those spirits wanted to enter pig bodies. He couldn't imagine anything worse than being a pig; ugly, smelly, dirty, and nothing to look forward to but ending up in someone's frying pan. He wanted to know why the spirits didn't want to go into the bodies of eagles, horses, or even dogs—anything but pigs.

"The obvious lesson here," he mused, "is that having a body, any body, is better than being just a spirit. But why pigs? A rat or a toad is better than a pig."

I thought about it a minute, but couldn't give him a good answer. Occasionally during the day the subject of the possessed pigs became the subject of our conversation, but we never really came up with any good explanations why the spirits preferred pigs over other animals.

We forgot all about pigs the next morning when our reading got us into *Luke 11:5-13*. A man goes to his friend's house at midnight to borrow three loaves of bread. He knocks and the friend responds:

> *Trouble me not: the door is now shut, and my children are with me in bed; I cannot rise and give thee.*

> Then Jesus says, *Though he will not rise and give him, because he is his friend, yet because of his importunity he will rise and give him as many as he needeth.*

As soon as we read this Elder Bateman had to know what importunity meant.

"It's like a little boy wanting a BB gun for Christmas," I explained. "His mother doesn't want him to have it because she is afraid he will shoot out his eye, but every single day between Thanksgiving and Christmas he tells his mom a BB gun is the only thing he wants for Christmas. That's importunity. The mother relents and buys the gun."

"Is importunity a bad thing?" he asks.

"Jesus doesn't say its either bad or good. It's just a way to get what you want," I explained. "It explains why the most ordinary guy sometimes marries the homecoming queen. She knows other guys who are smarter, richer and more handsome, but the ordinary guy camps on her doorstep and just won't leave her alone until she agrees to marry him. That's importunity."

"Because of importunity we keep tracting the same areas over and over again, hoping someone finally relents and lets us teach them," Bateman observed.

"Exactly right," I said.

I don't remember who came up with the next thought, but we quickly became very excited. We decided to conduct a little experiment to see if this *importunity* principle really worked. Some of the people we were teaching lived several miles out of town. We were putting a lot of miles on our bikes, and there were lots of hills. We didn't like arriving at appointments all sweaty from our vigorous bike riding, especially when we only bathed once a week.

As a general rule, district and zone leaders drove cars and motorbikes which we called mopeds, but the rank and file rode bicycles. We began to wonder if wise application of the *importunity principle* might get us a moped. We didn't dare hope for a car, but there were about five mopeds in the mission, and maybe, if we exercised enough *importunity* we could obtain one. These were low-to-the-ground, green machines, big enough for two missionaries to ride together. We needed only one.

Our plan was simple. We would start mentioning our need for a motorbike in our weekly reports to President Gardner. We wouldn't pester him, just offer timely and polite reminders of how much more work we could do, and additional people we could teach, if we were blessed with a moped. Each of us would bring up the subject in our weekly letters, and we would do it week after week after week until results were achieved. We would operate like dripping water, relentless and persistent, but nice.

Three weeks later some of the staff elders from the mission home showed up on our doorstep, delivering a new moped. Instead of taking one from a district or zone leader, President Gardner had bought us a new one. Wow! *Luke 11* had become one of our favorite chapters in the *New Testament*, and we had added the word *importunity* to our vocabularies forever.

Esslingen had a great ward, and it wasn't long until we had several families coming to church. The ward wasn't nearly as large as the one in Stuttgart, but just as active, a great place to bring new people.

One of the families we were teaching was *Bruder* and *Schwester* Kurtdogmus. He was from Turkey, working in Germany, and she was German, an artist. She painted historic scenes of Esslingen on plates and cups which were sold in tourist shops. They had a little girl about two, and lived with the mother-in-law who was listening to the discussions too. *Schwester* Kurtdogmus kept asking me to call her Heidi instead of *Schwester*, but that was against the rules. She was pretty. I'll never forget the third discussion. It was on an evening, in the middle of the week, about seven. We were a little late, even with a moped to speed us around, so I was in a hurry to set up the flannel board and begin. I hardly noticed that *Bruder* Kurtdogmus wasn't speaking to us, and didn't seem to want to participate in the discussion. The wife and mother-in-law weren't their usual happy selves either. The third discussion covered the *Word of Wisdom*, so I just assumed they were concerned about their tea, coffee, and cigarettes.

I had just begun the memorized part of the discussion when my mind suddenly went blank. As mentioned earlier I knew these discussions as well or better than anyone in the mission. If an elder said three or four words from any of the discussions, I immediately recognized where he was and could continue on from that spot. I could give any part of any discussion while doing pushups, cooking breakfast, or racing the moped through rush hour traffic. And none of this required any effort, like reciting your date of birth or social security number. But suddenly in the Kurtdogmus home my mind went blank. I asked Elder Bateman to adjust some of the figures on the flannel board while I gathered my thoughts.

In a short minute I was again plunging into the memorized part of the discussion for the second time. My mind went blank again. This time I was angry with myself. I had worked too hard to learn and remember the discussions to have this happen. What was wrong with my stupid memory? I would force myself to remember, or I would die trying. So I plunged ahead again, the things I had memorized finally coming back to me.

The discussion was not a success. Members of the family made very few comments, and had no questions. It soon became obvious they just wanted the lesson to end so they could get rid of us. I found out later that we had arrived while they were in the middle of a family fight over whether or not to continue the discussions. Our timing was bad, even though we had an appointment, and by being there we prevented them from resolving anything. Perhaps they wouldn't have resolved it anyway, but the way things worked out, the wife and mother-in-law continued taking the discussions, eventually being baptized, but the husband never met with us again.

As I thought about it, I began to wonder if I had been one to *blaspheme against the Holy Ghost*, the subject of the verse in *Mark 3*, Elder Bateman and I had been discussing a week or two earlier. I realized my mind had gone blank for a reason, not once but twice. The spirit had withdrawn. I had been wrong to push ahead with the discussion. I had been too insensitive to receive guidance from the Spirit of God. I had *blasphemed against the Holy Ghost*, a sin for which there might be no forgiveness. If I had listened to the spirit, and not given the lesson at that time, perhaps *Bruder* Kurtdogmus might have felt differently about us and the Church and been willing to continue the discussions with his family.

The thought occurred to me that my inability to find *a thousand souls* had more to do with my unwillingness to listen to the spirit than it had to do with the German people not wanting to learn about the Church. I was determined to try really hard to listen to that *still small voice* and pay a lot more attention to those feelings in my chest, the warm yearnings as well as the feelings of cold confusion, which seemed to be guides about what to do and where to go.

In spite of my shortcomings, the Lord was blessing us. It seemed every day we found someone new to teach. We were giving lots of discussions, and had half a dozen people committed to baptism. It was easy getting up in the morning, doing the usual fifty pushups, then reading the scriptures. It seemed our study time together was never long enough, because we were learning so much. Elder Bateman was making good progress with the lessons and the language. We got along well, and were working hard. This was the way missionary work is supposed to be, or so it seemed.

There was only one thing wrong. I started waking up in the middle of the night, unable to go back to sleep. I couldn't figure out what was causing my restlessness. Sometimes I would get out of bed, slip on my jeans and sneakers, and go out on the little deck overlooking the Neckar River. It was too cold to stay seated, so I would pace back and forth like an animal on the prowl. The following day I would feel a little tired, but that was all. I started going to bed a half-hour earlier to make up for the lost sleep.

FIFTEEN

One night when the moon was almost full, as I was pacing back and forth on the deck, my eye caught some movement on the stone bridge crossing the river. It wasn't a car or a bicycle, perhaps a person or animal. I stopped my pacing to get a better look. Now I couldn't see any movement, but I was sure I had seen something earlier. Like a deer hunter, I was patient, watching and waiting. I knew I had seen something. It would move again, and it did. A person was climbing up on the bridge railing. Then the person was leaning out, looking down into the black swirling depths. It was apparent that someone was about to commit suicide.

There was no time to wake Elder Bateman and wait for him to dress. I stepped over the balcony railing and lowered myself to the ground, and ran toward the bridge. It wasn't far, only a few hundred yards. From the entrance to the bridge I could see no one, not even in the moonlight. I hoped I wasn't too late as I raced to the spot where I had seen the person lean out from the railing.

He was still there. Or was it a she? All I could see was the back of a long, black coat. The stocking cap on the head was black too.

"Hey, better come back here before you fall," I said, trying to sound calm and nonthreatening.

The figure on the railing did not move.

"Go away." It was a man's voice. It sounded familiar.

"If you jump in, I'm coming after you. I'm not a good swimmer. Do you want to be responsible for my death too?"

"Go away."

"I'm not going away, so you might as well get off that railing."

There was silence for a minute. It appeared one of his hands was loosening its grip. "Don't do it," I said. "It's too nice of a night for this. Look at the moon on the water, the shadows on the church, the old city wall. It's a beautiful night. Don't make it ugly." I talked slowly, deliberately, calmly, trying to get him to think about what I was saying instead of what he wanted to do.

"There are no beautiful nights in my life, nor will there ever be. Go away. Please."

Now I knew who was speaking. I was sure of it. It was *Pfarr* Hermann.

"If you jump, the Catholic Church will lose a future pope," I said.

He turned and looked at me, recognizing my voice and face for the first time.

"You deceived and tricked all those people in Stuttgart. How could a man like you know anything about me?"

"I know you are one of Heavenly Father's great ones. I know it is wrong for you to jump from this bridge."

"You don't know anything," he said as he turned away from me to look down at the water. He let go of the rail and disappeared from sight.

Just like that, he was gone. He didn't yell or scream. I

could hear the splash. I remembered promising him that I would come in after him. Without thinking, I ran to the downstream side of the bridge, vaulted the railing and descended into the water. To my surprise, it wasn't very deep. My feet hit bottom, allowing me to push myself to the surface, where I treaded water, facing upsteam, looking for *Pfarr* Hermann. The water was clear and the moon was full. I saw him, his arms flailing against the current, gasping for air. He was not very far away. I swam to him, grabbed his coat collar, then started side-stroking toward shore. I wasn't an olympic swimmer, but I had passed my life-saving merit badge and knew what to do. I had been riding a bike most of my mission and my legs were strong.

I hadn't pulled him more than a few feet when one of my feet struck a rock. As the current carried us away from the bridge, the stream was getting shallower. Soon I was standing up, helping the coughing, gasping priest stand up too. Arm in arm we waded to shore.

"I feel so foolish," he said when we reached the rocky shore.

"Me too," I said.

"Why do you feel foolish?" he asked. "You have done a very brave thing."

"I feel foolish because the water is not deep. You would not have drowned. I didn't need to save you." We both began to laugh. I invited him to come to the missionary flat where we could change into some dry clothes before deciding what to do next. He did not resist. Arm in arm we returned to the flat.

We greeted the sunrise dressed in sweat clothes,

reclining in deck chairs on the balcony. Inside, Elder Bateman was busy with his study, and rustling up a few things for breakfast. Our wet clothing was hanging over the balcony railing to dry.

"I suppose you would like to give me one of your silly discussions," he said.

"First, I would rather know why the most popular priest in all Germany wants to take his life."

"You wouldn't understand."

"You're probably right about that. The worst thing that ever happened in my life was that article you helped place in the *Stuttgarter Zeitung*. But as bad as that was I didn't want to kill myself."

"That's good," he said.

"So what in your life is so much worse than that? You see yourself as God's servant. People love you. Wherever you go, congregations fill to capacity. I'm sure other priests are very envious of you."

"I have taken an oath of celibacy, for life."

"Now I can see why you want to kill yourself," I said. We both laughed, but humor was soon forgotten.

"I love my church and willingly accepted celibacy," he said. "But now I love a woman too. The Bishop found out. Like you, I was banished from Stuttgart. They sent me here until they decide what to do with me. They will probably send me to some remote corner of the world, maybe South Africa or Las Vegas."

I remembered *Bruder* Zander coming to the train station to express his frustrations over unfulfilled love. Now it was *Pfarr* Hermann. I wish I had more experience with these kind of things so I could be a better counselor.

"Have you talked to the woman about it? Does she know how you feel?"

"Such talk is forbidden."

"Not for her."

"Yes it is. She is a nun. I can't eat. I can't sleep. I have never felt anything so strong. I am overwhelmed, out of control. Sometimes thoughts enter my mind which a priest has no business thinking. I want to die."

"Wow," I said, "And I thought I had unresolved issues."

"You know her."

I remembered some of the more attractive sisters who had accompanied *Schwester* Frieda to some of our meetings. I wondered which one it might be.

"Frieda Busch. You call her *Schwester* Frieda."

"No wonder you jumped from the bridge. Her goodness is part of her beauty."

"Do you really think so?"

"Of course," I said, reaching into the pocket of my coat which was hanging over the chair. I pulled out a small, torn piece of brown butcher paper and handed it to him.

He looked at it cautiously. "This is her address," he said, astonished. "Why is it in your pocket?"

"I should have thrown it out when she betrayed me," I said. "But I couldn't do it. I guess I was hoping that someday I would write to her, and maybe get together after my mission, convince her to withdraw from the order."

"So we are rivals," he said, a gleam in his eye. I was glad he seemed to be feeling better. He reached out to hand the scrap of paper back to me. I didn't take it from him.

"No, you keep it. I am not your rival. I confess a strong attraction to *Schwester* Frieda, but I am not smitten like you are. I withdraw from your perceived rivalry." He folded the paper in half and held it tightly in his fist.

"Why is it you missionaries are so strong in resisting attractions to the opposite sex? Is there some word of advice you can give a struggling priest?"

"I think the only difference between you and me is that I know my period of celibacy will end after my mission. Perhaps I have learned discipline and self control, but when I return to Utah I will court and marry, with the blessing of the church. I feel sorry for you poor devils who are cursed with celibacy for life. That is not healthy. I am amazed that more of you don't jump from bridges. Nuns too."

"So you can't give me counsel on how to remain on course?"

"I can give you some very good counsel, but I don't think you are ready to hear it."

"Try me."

I stood up and started pacing back and forth, gathering my thoughts. The priest remained in his chair. Elder Bateman was somewhere inside the flat where I couldn't see him.

"First of all, I don't think it was an accident that *Schwester* Frieda crossed your path. I don't think it was an accident that both of us were sent to Esslingen at the same time. I believe the Lord has a hand in all this."

"You cannot convert me to your Mormon beliefs," he said.

"I know that, but I'd like you to close your eyes and try to imagine the scene I am about to describe."

"Okay." He closed his eyes.

"Imagine yourself a Mormon, just for a minute. You tell your bishop how you feel about *Schwester* Frieda. Instead of sending you off to Las Vegas or South Africa, he advises you to marry her, if she feels the same way about you. To do that you take her to the temple in Switzerland where dressed in white you kneel across an alter, holding hands, looking into each others' eyes as you are married, not just for time, but for all eternity."

"Stop it," he said, opening his eyes. "You are only making me more miserable, this picture of something I can never have."

"Think of it this way," I said, pushing forward. "If the Catholic Church is right, the best you can ever hope for in life, is banishment to South Africa or Las Vegas, where you will never see *Schwester* Frieda again. If the Mormon Church is true, *Schwester* Frieda will share your life for the rest of eternity. You will have to learn to paint houses, fix cars or teach school because the church will not give you money, but through its priesthood it will bestow on you and *Schwester* Frieda the blessings of Abraham. You'll be partners in Christ in an eternal family with sons, daughters, grandchildren, great grand children—a posterity as numerous as the sands of the seashore. I'll bet you can't look me in the eye and tell me that is wrong, or that you don't want something like that."

"Stop it."

"No. If there is only one chance in a million that I am right and you are wrong, isn't it worth checking out? Isn't the thing my church offers you a billion times more precious than what your church can give you?"

"How do I get past the foolishness—gold plates that are hidden in a mountain, stories of a fourteen-year-old boy walking and talking with God, people who believe God can bless them with many wives?"

"You can start by reading our *Book of Mormon*. It contains stories of men like you who wrestled to find the truth, and were successful. Enos prayed all night. Alma was struck down by angels in finding the right way. A King Lamoni lost consciousness until those around him thought he was dead.

While I was speaking, I looked him in the eye, speaking deliberately, pausing frequently, letting the words settle in his mind. I knew I was speaking the truth, and believed he was hearing it, words like sharpened butcher knives sinking to the center of his heart.

"As you read these stories you will feel warm stirrings in your heart, telling you they are true, and that they have meaning for you. At the end of the book there is a promise that if you do certain things, God will give you your own personal manifestation about the truthfulness of these things. You don't have to believe anything I say. Your confirmation that these things are true will come directly from God."

"I don't know."

"I believe the reason all this happened tonight, both of us coming to Esslingen, our meeting on the bridge, jumping in the river... all this happened because God wants you and Frieda to be together. It can't happen the way things are today. I am helping God point you in the right direction." I got up from my chair, and went inside to find *Pfarr* Hermann a brand new *Book of Mormon.*

"When you read this you will know I am telling the truth," I said as I handed it to him. He took the book, grabbed his wet clothes, and headed out the front door.

When he was gone, Elder Bateman asked how we were going to write in our report that we took time swimming in the river and talking with *Pfarr* Hermann.

"Proselyting time, of course," I said. "I taught him the seventh discussion."

"We don't have a seventh discussion."

"We do now. It's called *Eternal Marriage.*"

"What do you want for breakfast? It's my turn to cook."

"Nothing. We're fasting. Today, tomorrow, and probably the next day too."

"For *Pfarr* Hermann?"

"Yes. While he reads the *Book of Mormon.*"

"Should we tell the president you went swimming?"

"I didn't go swimming. I was practicing baptism by immersion with a man through whom *a thousand souls* will find the truth, if not through his immediate sphere of influence, at least through his posterity."

EPILOGUE

We had finished our food a long time ago, and the waitress had removed the dirty dishes. All that was left were the two fortune cookies on a small plate. I picked up one of them and began to break it open.

"I assume he read the *Book of Mormon*," Mr. Crandall said.

"Yes he did. He loved the stories. He had a million questions. When they kicked him out of the monastery we helped him buy new clothes. He found a part-time job at the local library. In the fall he is returning to the university at Tübingen to finish his training to be a history teacher. I baptized him the week before I left Esslingen."

"And *Schwester* Frieda?"

"She was more of a challenge. She thought he had gone crazy. She refused to see him. At first our only contact with her was letters. We both wrote to her, but she did not write back, at least not at first. Eventually she agreed to a meeting—with him, me, and my companion—in that same park where she copied the letter to Elder Cook."

I closed my eyes, remembering that sunny summer afternoon. The three of us were sitting on a park bench, facing in the direction of the cloister, waiting. . . .

"What happened? Did she come?"

"Yes. When she walked into sight, entering the park, I

looked at her, then at Bruder Hermann. I don't remember their first words to each other, but I'll never forget what I learned that afternoon."

"And what might that be?"

"That when people are in love it shows."

"Like how?"

"The lightness of her step. The way he fumbled his words. The way they looked at each other. Their reluctance to end the meeting, long after our business was finished, and a hundred other things. We gave her a *Book of Mormon* again. She promised to read and pray. Many more letters were exchanged. She returned to her family to fight the old conversion battles with parents and friends. Now she is ready to be baptized too, and she wants me to do it. After the baptism, I will be the best man at the wedding."

"You are leaving out something," Mr. Crandall said. "You mentioned helping bless a baby. Is there a matter of repentance that *Schwester* Frieda and *Bruder* Hermann need to be concerned about? Not even the Catholic Church would condone a priest-nun relationship resulting in a child."

"No, no, no," I laughed. "The baby belongs to *Bruder* and *Schwester* Zander. Remember? The gospel doctrine teacher and *Whatshername*. He took her to dinner like he promised to do at the train station. A month later they were engaged, then married. Now they have a baby and want me to help bless it."

"And what about Elder Kimball's promise? How many did you baptize?"

"Not a thousand, not a hundred, or even close to that. But when I think about *Bruder* and *Schwester* Hermann, *Bruder* and *Schwester* Zander, these new couples, their spheres of influence, and their posterity through three or four generations, there's going to be a lot more than *a thousand souls* touched by the events in the story you heard today. I no longer worry that Elder Kimball was out of line when he made that promise."

"I suppose we should go back to the bank and sign the papers," Crandall said, starting to get up from the table.

"Wait," I said. "We forgot the fortune cookies."

I opened mine.

Even a tiny pebble tossed on still waters can cause a thousand ripples.

AUTHOR'S NOTE

Whenever I tell a story like this I receive letters and e-mails asking how much of it is really true. Yes, I left the Berkeley campus of the University of California to go on a thirty-month mission to Southern Germany in 1962. Yes, Elder Kimball blessed me to bring the truth to a thousand souls.

I didn't keep a daily journal, but I think my memory is sound. I estimate about ninety percent of the events described in this story really happened, pretty much as I remember them, or perhaps as I wish I remember them. After forty years, I'm sure some of the events are out of order. Some of the names and places are probably mixed up too, though sometimes intentionally to help the flow of the story. Sometimes name and place changes were deliberate to avoid reaction from those who may not approve their role in the event described. For those whose names I have not changed, if there is any offense, I apologize.

I understand that others who were there may remember these events somewhat differently. Human memory is selective and subjective, at best, especially after forty years of elapsed time. Therefore to avoid any potential arguments, I simply declare this book a novel, a work of fiction, but not in the ordinary sense. Since most of the events really did happen to me—mostly as I remember them—the label that best describes this work is *autobiographical novel*. If there is not already a body of literature fitting this category, then let this be the first.

Lee Nelson Books by Mail

All mail-order books are personally autographed by Lee Nelson.

The Storm Testament, 291 pages, $14.95.

Wanted by Missouri law for his revenge on mob leader Dick Boggs in 1839, fifteen-year-old Dan Storm flees to the Rocky Mountains with his friend, Ike, an escaped slave. Dan settles with the Ute Indians where he courts the beautiful Red Leaf. Ike becomes chief of a band of Gosiutes in Utah's west desert. All this takes place before the arrival of the Mormon pioneers.

The Storm Testament II, 293 pages, $14.95.

In 1845 a beautiful female journalist, disguised as a schoolteacher, sneaks into the Mormon city of Nauvoo to lure the polygamists out of hiding so the real story on Mormon polygamy can be published to the world. What Caroline Logan doesn't know is that her search for truth will lead her into love, blackmail, Indian raids, buffalo stampedes, and a deadly early winter storm on the Continental Divide in Wyoming.

The Storm Testament III, 268 pages, $14.95.

Inspired by business opportunities opened up by the completion of the transcontinental railroad in 1870, Sam Storm and his friend, Lance Claw, attempt to make a quick fortune dealing in firewater and stolen horses. A bizarre chain of events involves Sam and the woman he loves in one of the most ruthless schemes of the 19th Century.

The Storm Testament IV, 278 pages, $14.95.

Porter Rockwell recruits Dan Storm in a daring effort to stop U.S. troops from invading Utah in 1857, while the doomed Fancher Company is heading south to Mountain Meadows. A startling chain of events leads Dan and Ike into the middle of the most controversial and explosive episode in Utah history, the Mountain Meadow Massacre.

The Storm Testament V, 335 pages, $14.95.

Gunning for U.S. marshals and establishing a sanctuary for pregnant plural wives, Ben Storm declares war on the anti-Mormon forces of the 1880's. The United States Government is determined to bring the Mormon Church to its knees, with polygamy as the central issue. Ben Storm fights back.

Rockwell, 443 pages, $14.95.

The true story of the timid farm boy from New York who became the greatest gunfighter in the history of the American West. He drank his whiskey straight, signed his name with an X, and rode the fastest horses, while defending the early Mormon prophets.

Walkara, 353 pages, $14.95.

The true story of the young savage from Spanish Fork Canyon who became the greatest horse thief in the history of the American West, the most notorious slave trader on the western half of a continent, the most wanted man in California, and the undisputed ruler over countless bands of Indians and a territory larger than the state of Texas. But his toughest challenge of all was to convince a beautiful Shoshone woman to become his squaw.

Cassidy, 440 pages, $16.95.

The story of the Mormon farm boy from Southern Utah who put together the longest string of successful bank and train robberies in the history of the American West. Unlike most cowboy outlaws of his day, Butch Cassidy defended the poor and oppressed, refused to shoot people, and shared his stolen wealth with those in need.

Storm Gold, 276 pages, $14.95.

In his quest for gold, Victorio Del Negro takes on the entire Ute Nation, and loses. A historical novel bringing to life the early Spanish history of the Rocky Mountain West, before the arrival of the Mormons.

Wasatch Savage, 135 pages, $17.95

An athletic boy from Spanish Fork sets out to become a world champion bull rider. A disillusioned inventor disappears into the ragged Wasatch mountains in search of meaning and purpose. This is a story of searching, conflict, romance and superhuman achievement.

Dance of Courage, 105 pages, $8.95.

A compilation of Lee Nelson's favorite short stories, including Dance of Courage, Abraham Webster's Last Chance, Stronger than Reason, and The Sure Thing.

Send orders to:

Cedar Fort, Incorporated
925 North Main St.
Springville, Utah 84663

You can also order by calling toll-free at 1-800-SKYBOOK or by ordering directly from our website at **www.cedarfort.com**

Include $3.49 shipping & handling for the first book, then 99 cents shipping for each additional book.